TALLAHASSEE felt as if she were going mad, or had passed the border of sanity during the time that the rod had drawn her on.

The stranger before her lay face down. With an effort she rolled the body over. She was sure somehow that this was death. But as the other's face came into view, Tallahassee screamed and flinched away.

Save for the slight difference in the color of their skins, the artificially lengthened, darkened brows and the headband that rose in front to the likeness of a striking serpent—she was looking down at the same features she saw every time she stood before a mirror!

"NORTON . . . AT HER BEST!"
                    —*Publishers Weekly*

WRAITHS
OF
TIME

a
novel
by

Andre Norton

A FAWCETT CREST BOOK • NEW YORK

For *Esther Turner, Renee Damone,* and *Carol Cross,*
all of whom have had their own struggles to prove
themselves against odds in a hostile world.

WRAITHS OF TIME

THIS BOOK CONTAINS THE COMPLETE TEXT OF THE
ORIGINAL HARDCOVER EDITION.

Published by Fawcett Crest Books, a unit of CBS Publications,
the Consumer Publishing Division of CBS Inc., by arrangement
with Atheneum

ISBN: 0-449-23532-7

Printed in the United States of America

10 9 8 7 6 5 4 3 2 1

THE box was placed in the exact center of the desk. Under the full beam of light Jason Robbins had turned on it, its eighteen inches of age-yellowed ivory glowed as might polished wood. Or was she only imagining that, Tallahassee wondered. This artifact had a quality of—she searched for the right word, then knew it was one she would not use aloud—enchantment, that was it. There was a golden inlay on the lid, as well as four other disks, inlaid with gold, one on each side. She could guess without touching that they had been fashioned of that pure, soft gold used in ancient times.

"Well"—the grey-haired man, apparently in charge here, leaned forward a little—"can you give us any lead, Miss Mitford?"

Tallahassee found difficulty in turning away from the box at which she had stared from the moment Jason had snapped on the desk lamp.

"I don't know." She spoke the truth. "There are elements of African design, yes. See." She pointed a finger, nearly as ivory in color as the time-darkened box itself, at the gold inlay on the lid which formed a strip curved like a snake to travel the length of the ivory. Yet the spiral had no real head, rather there was a strip of precious metal bent at right angles—not unlike a stylized hunting knife. "That really combines two known devices of old kingship. This device at the top is the 'plow' which we believe was carried by the rulers of Meroë. The rest is of a later period, perhaps, a symbolic sword blade in the form of a snake. But these two forms have never, to my knowledge, been found so linked before. The Meroë dynasties borrowed greatly from Egypt, and there the snake was a sign of royalty, usually a part of the crown. These"—her finger moved to the disks at the sides—"are again symbolic. They resemble very closely those gold badges that were worn by the 'soul-washers' of the Ashanti, the attendants of the king whose duty it was to ward off any danger of contamination from general evil. Yet—though it combines symbols from two, maybe three periods of African history, it is very old—"

"Would you say a museum piece then?" The man Jason had introduced as Roger Nye persisted. His tone was impatient, as if he had expected some instant snap judgment from her. And his tone aroused in Tallahassee her own, sometimes militant, stubbornness.

"Mr. Nye, I am a student of archaeology, employed at present to help catalogue the Lewis Brooke collection. There are many tests that would have to be made to date this artifact, tests for which one needs certain equipment. But I will say that the workmanship . . ." She paused before she asked a question of her own:

"Have you seen the rod of office in the Brooke collection?"

"What's that got to do with it? Or are you saying that

this"—Nye indicated the box—"could be a part of that collection?"

"If it is," she was careful in her answer, "it was not included in the official customs inventory. However, there is something . . ." Tallahassee shook her head. "You do not want guesses, you want certainties. Dr. Roman Carey will be here tonight. He is coming to study the collection. I would advise you to let him see this. At present he is the greatest authority on art of the Sudan."

"You are sure it is Sudanese?" Now it was Jason who asked the question.

Tallahassee made a small gesture. "I told you, I cannot be sure of anything. I would say it is old, very old. As to its general point of origin I would believe Africa. But the combination of symbols I have not seen before. If I may . . ." She put out a hand toward the box, only to have Nye's hand close tightly about her wrist in a lightning-quick movement.

She looked at him in open amazement and then irritated dislike.

"You don't understand." Jason broke in again, speaking very swiftly as if he were afraid she could keep no better rein on her temper now than she could when they were children. "The thing is hot!"

"Hot?"

"It radiates some form of energy." Nye studied her with those measuring eyes. "That was how it was found, really. It was by sheer chance." He freed her hand, and she jerked it back to her lap. "One of our field men went to put his kit in a locker at the airport. He had a geiger counter with him and it started to register. He was quick to use it and located the source of radiation in a nearby locker. Then he called me. We got the port key for the locker. This was the only thing inside."

"Radioactive," Tallahassee murmured. "But how . . . "

Nye shook his head. "Not atomic, though a counter can pick it up. It's something new, but the lab boys did not want to take it to pieces—"

"I should say not!" Tallahassee was thoroughly aroused at the suggestion of such vandalism. "It may be unique. Has it been opened?"

Nye shook his head. "There is no visible fastening. And it seemed better not to handle it too much until we were sure of what we had. Now what about this rod of office you mentioned, what is it and where was it found?"

"There was a strong belief in the old African kingdoms that the soul of a nation could be enclosed in some precious artifact. The Ashanti war with England a hundred years ago came about because an English governor demanded the King's stool to sit on as a sign of the transferral of rulership. But even the King could not sit on that. Sitting on a floor mat, he might only lean a portion of his arm upon it while making some very important decree or when assuming the kingship. To the Ashanti people the stool contained the power of all the tribal ancestors and was holy; it possessed a deeply religious as well as a political significance—which the English did not attempt to find out before they made their demands.

"Other tribes had similar symbols of divine contact with their ancestors and their gods. Sometimes at the death of a king such symbols were retired to a special house from which they were brought to 'listen' when there was need for a grave change in some law or the demand for a decision involving the future of the people as a whole. These artifacts were very precious, and among some tribes were never seen at all except by priests or priestesses.

"The rod of office which Lewis Brooke found is believed to be one of these tokens. And because he discovered it in a place that has some very odd legends, it is of double value."

"He found it in the Sudan then?"

"No, much farther west. It was nearer to Lake Chad. There is an old legend that when the Arab-Ethiopian kingdom of Axum overran Meroë, the royal clan—and they themselves were the descendents of Egyptian Pharaohs and held jealously to much of the very ancient beliefs—fled west and were supposed to have established a refuge near Lake Chad. There has never been any real proof of this, not until Doctor Brooke made his spectacular find—an unplundered tomb containing many artifacts and a sarcophagus, though the latter was empty, and there was evidence that no body had ever been within it. Instead the rod of office rested there."

"The soul of the nation buried," Jason said softly.

Tallahassee nodded. "Perhaps. There were inscriptions, but, though they used Egyptian hieroglyphics, the later Meroë tongue has never been translated so they could not be deciphered. Dr. Brooke's unfortunate accidental death last year has delayed the work on the whole project of arranging and identifying the artifacts."

"I am surprised," Nye commented, "that he was allowed to take anything out of the country to bring here. The new nations are doubly jealous of losing any of their treasures—especially to us."

"We were surprised, too," Tallahassee admitted. "But he had full permission." She hesitated and then added: "There was something odd about the whole matter, as if they wanted to get rid of all the finds for some reason of their own."

Jason's eyes narrowed. "A threatened uprising, perhaps, using the old rod of office for a rallying point?"

Nye's attention swung from the girl to the young man. "You believe that?"

Jason shrugged. "Rebellions have been started on

lesser excuses. Remember the Ashanti and their stool."

"But you say yourself that was a hundred years ago!" Nye protested.

"Africa is very old. It has seen the rise and fall of three waves of civilization—maybe more for who has actually identified those who ruled at Zimbabwe or in the intricate fortifications of Iyanga? Men remember well in Africa. The later kings might not have any scribes, but just like the Celtic lords of Europe who had no written language, they had trained memory banks among their own kind—men who could stand up in council and recite facts, genealogies, laws reaching back three and four hundred years. Such skills do not die easily among such people."

Inwardly Tallahassee was ready to laugh. Jason was drawing on her own knowledge now, though he had often enough in the past shrugged at her comments and conversation as being deadly dull. Who cared what happened two thousand years ago anyway? The best time was here and now.

"Hmmm." Nye leaned back in the chair behind the desk. He was not focusing on either of the young people, nor even on the box now. Instead his eyes were half-closed as if he were thinking deeply.

Tallahassee broke that moment of silence. "I would suggest—" she said boldly. After all no one had made plain just what this Nye's authority was in the matter (though she judged from Jason's hurried call which had first brought her here that he was some VIP of the type who is never identified publicly, if he can help it). "I would suggest that you put that"—she gestured at the box—"in the museum safe. There is perhaps only one man, Dr. Carey, who can make a true identification if that is what you need."

Nye opened his eyes wide then in a long stare turned on her, as if he could unlock her thoughts by merely looking at her intently. The girl lifted her chin a fraction of an inch and met his gaze with one as steady.

"All right," he decided. "And I want to see this 'rod' of yours into the bargain. But not right now. We've got to think about who planted this—*here*. Robbins, you go with her . . ." He glanced at the watch on his wrist.

"It's nearly closing time for the museum, I take it. Better make it fast—we don't want any action which can be noted as out of the ordinary, not if this thing has any political overtones."

He had brought out a briefcase, snapped it open. To Tallahassee's surprise the interior had been metal lined. Now Nye produced a pair of tongs from the inner cover of the case and used them to slide the box into it. As Tallahassee stood up, Nye handed the case to Robbins.

"Yes, it's lead-lined, Miss Mitford. We're taking no chances about the radiation, even if it is a new one to us. Robbins had better carry this. When does Carey get in?"

"He should be there already."

"Good enough. Ask him to call this number"—Nye scrawled some figures on a card and pushed it to her—"as soon as he can. And thank you, Miss Mitford. Put the case and its contents in the safe. Robbins will drive you."

He turned to pick up a phone as if Tallahassee had already dissolved into thin air. The girl waited until the door of the office had closed behind them before she spoke again.

"Who's that playing James Bond?"

Jason shook his head. "Don't ask me, girl. All I know is that the Big Chief himself couldn't get better service if he showed his face in these parts. I'm small fry, but I got asked in 'cause somewhere along the line since that was found yesterday somebody said, 'Oh, my, now just maybe that's African!' I guess then somebody went and asked the computer who locally could tell them the truth and I got punched out. But I saw it wasn't modern—so I called you."

"Jason, do you really think this *is* political? I know that finding the rod in the sarcophagus was odd, and it does make some sense about it being a 'soul' burial. But this thing . . ."

"It was you, Tally, my dear, who tied this to your rod, remember?"

"Because there is something alike in them"—she watched him stow the heavy case in the car—"only I can't just put a finger to it. It's more a feeling than anything else." She bit her lip. There she went again, one of her hunches. Someday she was going to be proved very wrong, and when she was—

"One of those feelings of yours, eh?" Jason's left eyebrow slid up. "Still having them?"

"Well, a lot of times they've paid off!" Tallahassee retorted. "You know they have."

"You've been lucky," was Jason's verdict as he edged the car into the heavy traffic of the beginning rush hour. "Will we make it before they close up that repository of dead knowledge for the night?"

"They close to the public at four, but the back door is for staff and I have a key. The alarms won't go on until Hawes has made sure everyone is out of the offices and that those are shut for the night. Dr. Carey should be there."

Jason concentrated on his driving, Tallahassee was content to sit quietly. She tried to understand the odd emotion inside of her which she had been aware of ever since she had gotten into the car. Twice she had actually turned her head to glance into the narrow back seat of Jason's bug. No one there. Yet the sensation of another presence was growing so acute it made her nervous, and she had to exert more and more control not to squirm around again and again.

The thought was strong in her now that what they carried was important. Not, she believed, exactly for the reasons that the mysterious Mr. Nye might think, but for some other reason. That was probably her "hunch" busy working overtime, and she tried to dismiss all thought of what they carried, of the museum even. Her vacation—it started next Monday. She had had to wait for the coming of Dr. Carey . . .

Not that it was a real vacation and she was going to utterly escape her job. But to fly to Egypt and join the Matraki party! Egypt–Meroë . . . She could not keep her thoughts on vacation plans. That nagging feeling persisted. But she was not going to give in to it!

The traffic was lighter now as Jason swung off the expressway and started through the series of streets to get to the museum. It was darker than usual—a lot of clouds piling up—maybe a storm later on.

When the car pulled into the narrow back way used by delivery trucks, Tallahassee got out quickly. She had fitted in her key and had the door open when Jason followed her, his arm dragged down under the weight of the case.

"Who's there?" There was a light only at the far end of the hall, and it seemed twice as dark as usual.

Then the upper lights flashed on, and she could see the chief guard.

"Oh, you, Miss Mitford. 'Bout ready to lock up."

"We have something for the safe, Mr. Hawes. This is my cousin, Mr. Robbins. He's with the FBI here."

"Saw your picture, Mr. Robbins, in the paper last week. That sure was a good haul you fellows made, pickin' up all them drug smugglers."

Jason smiled. "The boss says just routine. But I'm glad that the public appreciates our efforts now and then."

"Did Dr. Carey come?" Tallahassee wanted to get

rid of that case, put the building and this day out of her life for now.

"Yes, ma'am. He's in that extra office of Dr. Greenley's, fifth floor. The back elevator's on, faster for you than the stairs."

"I left my car just out there," Jason pointed. "Be back as quick as I can."

"That's all right, Mr. Robbins. Nobody'll bother it there."

Tallahassee hurried around a corner and into an elevator. Jason had to take long strides to keep up with her.

"You're in a rush all of a sudden," he commented.

"I want to get that in the safe," she said with an emphasis she regretted a moment later when again his left eyebrow arose in question.

"Well," she added in her own defense, "I can't help what I feel. There—there's something wrong."

She saw the eyes in Jason's brown face go suddenly sober.

"All right. I'll accept your hunch as real. This has been a queer one from the start. Where's this safe?"

"In Dr. Greenley's office."

"There's one thing—don't forget to tell this Carey about Nye wanting to hear from him."

She had almost forgotten Nye; now she hoped she could find that card in her purse. The urgency that gripped her had absolutely no base in anything but her nerves. But she felt if she did not manage to get rid of the case and out of here something dreadful *was* going to happen. And so acute was that feeling she dared not let Jason know the force of it. He would think she had lost her mind.

In the fifth floor the hall lights were still on, and their footsteps on the marble floor were audible. But Tallahassee found herself straining to pick up another sound, perhaps a third set of heel taps. That belief—no, it could not be a belief—that they had an invisible companion was intensifying. Tallahassee caught her lower lip between her teeth and held it so, using all her self-control to keep her eyes straight ahead, refusing to look over her shoulder where nothing could possibly be.

She reached the door of the director's office with a sigh of relief and pulled it open, her hand reaching out to snap on the light switch. Before that gesture was completed she gave a little cry. Then a burst of light filled the room to display how silly she had been. Of course no one had passed her. There was no one here but herself and Jason, who was now closing the door behind them.

"What is it?" he demanded.

Tallahassee forced a laugh. "I guess it is all this secret business. I thought I saw a shadow move . . ."

"Only the Shadow knows . . ." intoned Jason solemnly. "You *are* nervy tonight, Tally. Get your work done, and I'll take you out for dinner."

"Some place cheerful," she found herself saying, "with lots of lights—"

"I beg your pardon."

With another gasp Tallahassee swung around. The inside door between this and the neighboring office had opened. A slender man who must be at least an inch or so shorter than herself—which was not unusual: when a girl stands five-eleven-and-a-half shoeless, she does not look up to many males—was eyeing her in manifest disapproval.

He was thin featured, his nose sharp-pointed, his mouth turning down with a sour twist. And his sandy hair had been combed back with care over a pink scalp, which showed only too readily through those thin strands, to touch his collar in the back.

"I believe this is Dr. Greenley's office—" His thin lips shaped each word as if he broke them off as he spoke them.

"I am Tallahassee Mitford, Dr. Greenley's assistant in the African division."

He surveyed her, Tallahassee realized, with actual distaste, and she could sense his resentment. Was he one of those who disliked and downgraded any woman with a pretense of knowledge in their own field? She had met several of that ilk.

"You are quite young," he commented in a way which made the observation vaguely offensive. "But surely you are aware that this place is not a proper one for social contacts."

He had looked beyond her at Jason. And if he was implying what she thought he was—Tallahassee had to subdue her flaring temper with every bit of control she could muster. After all, she would have to work with this man (whether either of them liked it or not) until the Brooke collection was catalogued.

"We have something to put in the safe." She hated herself for even explaining that much, but she knew she had to. "And—" She opened her purse. For once luck was with her. That card was right on top, and she did not have to waste any time delving around in sometimes jumbled floating contents to find it. "I was given this. It is for you to call as soon as possible."

She laid the card down on the edge of Dr. Greenley's overflowing desk and did not look at the man again as she went to the safe. As long as Hawes had not yet snapped on the night alarms she could open it.

Jason, his mouth set in a way she well knew (he had his own temper, even if he had learned long ago how to keep it under), came around the other side of the desk with the case ready. She did not know nor care at the moment whether Dr. Carey had his precious phone number or not. As the door came open at her pull Jason slipped the case in. Tallahassee slammed the door, spun the dial. Still ignoring Dr. Carey, she walked to the phone and punched the number of Dr. Greenley's home.

"Is Dr. Joe in?" she asked as she heard Mrs. Greenley's deep, pleasant voice. "Yes, it's Tally. Oh. Well, when he comes in, tell him there's something in the safe. It was picked up—by the FBI."

She had Jason's nod to reassure her that she could keep to that story.

"Yes. They want an opinion on it. They'll contact him tomorrow. No, I don't know much more. But it's terribly important. No, I'm not going home right away—Jason's in town and we're going to eat out. Thank you. I'll ask him. Good-bye."

She set the phone down and smiled with angry brightness at Jason. "Mrs. Greenley says if you have time before you leave, do stop in and see her. Now"—she swung back to the man who had made no attempt not to listen in—"you have the reason for my being here, Dr. Carey. If you care to check on me, you need only call the Greenleys."

"Not so fast," he said, as she turned away. "As you have been working on the Brooke files, I want you here the first thing in the morning. They must be completely rechecked, of course."

"Oh course," Tallahassee said softly. "You have your own methods of working—"

"I certainly do!" he snapped.

It came to her that he was watching her with a kind of outrage—as if the mere fact that she existed and must be a part of his daily round in the future was an insult which he found hard to bear. And his hostility was so patent that she began to lose her own control, but also grew curious at what had so forcibly triggered this seemingly instant dislike for her.

As she and Jason went down in the elevator she was

aware of something else. That feeling of a third person was gone, even her queer hunch was fading. Maybe she had left it all back in the safe and, if it did have any effect, let it bother Dr. Carey—it might do him some good.

$\mathcal{T}$ALLAHASSEE sighed contentedly and Jason laughed.

"For a black chick you sure do put away a Chinese dinner in a competent manner," he commented.

"I like Foo Kong's, I like sweet-sour pork, I like—"

"Fortune cookies?" He broke open one and unrolled the paper slip inside with the air of a judge about to pronounce sentence.

"Well, well, this is apt enough. 'Food cures hunger, study cures ignorance.' What weighty thought lies in yours?"

Tallahassee produced her own. "That's odd . . ."

"What's odd? They put the bill for this feast in yours, Tally?"

"No," she answered a little absently and read: "Dragon begets Dragon, Phoenix begets Phoenix."

"I don't see anything odd about that. Just another way of saying 'like begets like.' "

"It could have another meaning, too. The dragon was the Emperor's symbol—no one else dared use it. And the phoenix was that of the Empress. It could mean that royalty begets only royalty."

"Which is just what I said, isn't it?" queried Jason, watching her intently.

"I don't know—oh, I guess it is." But why had she had that odd momentary feeling that the message of a fortune cookie, which was simply some old proverb, had a special significance for her?

"Look here, I didn't say anything because I had a hunch you didn't want to talk about it." Jason broke across her thought. "But what are you going to do about this Carey. It's plain he's going to make a brute of himself if he can. I wonder why?"

Tallahassee had tried to keep their encounter with Dr. Carey out of her mind all through dinner. But she would have to face it sooner or later, and she might as well do so now that Jason had brought it into the open.

"It could be," she returned frankly, "because I'm black. But I think mostly because I'm a woman. There're a lot of Ph.D.'s floating around, and not all of them are whites either, who resent any female daring to crowd into their own particular field. Which is one reason, my dear, that we're pushing for ERA—and you hear about Amazons giving the cry the matriarchy shall rise again! Oddly enough, matriarchy of a sort did persist, and right in Africa, too, for a long time. When a queen in Europe could be pushed around like a chesswoman on some plotter's board, queens well to the south were leading their own armies and wielding such influence as no white skin dared dream of. Each kingdom had three dominant women, if not more—the queen mother, not necessarily the ruling king's mother, but rather the most important royal woman of the preceding generation; the king's sister, because only she could produce a royal heir—the king's sons mostly didn't count; and his first wife. Why, in Ashanti, the king's wives had the duty of collecting all the taxes and had their own very efficient guards, attendants and the like, to do just that."

"So—if Carey is the expert on African history he's supposed to be," commented Jason, "he ought to know all this. Maybe that's why he wants to cut you down before you take over your natural-born rulership of his department. But"—Jason turned serious now—"look out for him, Tally. I think he could be an ugly customer if he sets out to be."

She nodded. "I know, and nothing can be deadlier than department politics. Luckily, Dr. Greenley has seen me work long enough to know what I can do. Jason, it's nearly nine thirty!" She had glanced at her watch.

"The knife flaying the elephant does not have to be large, only sharp!"

She gazed at Jason. "Now just what does *that* mean?"

"We had some wisdom of the East." He gestured to the discarded scraps from the cookies. "I was merely supplying some from our own native stock. In other words, watch your step."

"I'll probably be doing that so steadily I'll trip over my own feet," she agreed as she stood up. "The Greenleys are pets, I won't rock any boats to make trouble for Dr. Joe."

Jason was unlocking her apartment door for her when they heard the steady shrill of the telephone inside. "Oh!" She sent the door spinning with a hard push and crossed the dark living room in a rush to catch up the phone which gave one last demanding ring.

"Tallahassee?" It was Dr. Joe, and he sounded odd, his voice strained.

"Yes—"

"Thank goodness I got you. Can you come down right now to the museum? I wouldn't ask except it is of the utmost importance." Then the line clicked off so suddenly she stood there, startled. This was not Dr. Greenley's way . . .

"What is it?"

"Dr. Greenley." She put the phone down. "He just told me to come down to the museum—at this hour!—and hung up. Something's happened! It must have!"

"I'll take you." Jason moved behind her to shut the door, taking out the key to hand to her. She felt a little dazed. In her two years of work—first as a junior assistant, then as a full-fledged assistant—this had never happened. She could feel the uneasiness now even as she had felt that shadow of a third presence, which, of course, had never been there, accompanying her through the museum.

"There's something terribly wrong," she murmured as Jason settled beside her in the car and started to work his way out of the parking lot.

"Sure, that Carey," he returned.

But what could Dr. Carey have done or said to make Dr. Joe call her down to the museum at night? She could not think of anything and was still bewildered when Jason brought her to the same back door they had entered some hours earlier. There was a light in the hall now and just inside the door was Hawes. He swung it open.

"Go right on up, Miss Mitford. The elevator's waiting."

Jason had moved out but Tallahassee turned. "No, you stay here, Jas—if it's department business I'll do more than put a foot wrong to bring a stranger into it."

"You sure?" He looked both concerned and doubtful.

She nodded vigorously enough, she hoped, to satisfy him.

"I'm sure. And if it's going to be a long session I'll phone down and Mr. Hawes can tell you. I know you have to take the early plane out. That all right, Mr. Hawes?"

"Sure thing, Miss."

As Tallahassee entered the elevator, she half expected to feel that other presence. But there was nothing, except the rather eerie sensation that was always part of the museum when it was closed to the public and most of the staff was gone, intensified perhaps by the fact this was night. The storm which had promised earlier had not yet broken, but the sky outside was still overclouded and now she heard, even through the thickness of the walls about her, a roll of what could only be distant thunder.

Thunder of drums—somehow that phrase slipped into her mind as she shifted from one foot to the other impatiently, waiting for the elevator to reach the fifth floor. Drums meant so much in Africa—the famous "talking drums" whose expertly induced sounds could actually mimic tribal tongues so that they could be understood. . . .

The elevator door opened, and she looked into the open hall. There was a light on behind the frosted glass of Dr. Greenley's door. Tallahassee found herself breathing as swiftly as if she had been running. Deliberately she made herself walk more slowly. She was not going to burst into Dr. Joe's office as if she had been called from play like some forgetful child.

When she knocked and heard his muffled voice in answer, she worked to summon full control. And a moment later she was facing him across a desk that was no longer stacked with papers as it had been all the length of time she had known him. Those had been swept to the floor, a snowstorm of littered pages, books, magazines. The office was in such wild confusion that she halted just within the door and gasped. It could look no worse, she believed, if a small hurricane had gone to work here.

"What—what happened?"

Dr. Joe's jaw was set. "That's what we are trying to find out, Tallahassee. Someone was undoubtedly hunting something; to the best of my knowledge there was nothing here worth this effort."

"No?" That supercilious voice came from the corner. Dr. Carey sat on a chair, looking about him with a satisfaction he could not hide from Tallahassee's narrowed eyes. "Ask this Miss Mitford of yours what she and her boyfriend so conveniently locked in your safe tonight."

Dr. Joe did not even look at him. "Tallahassee, if you have any explanation at all of this, I would be grateful for it."

Tallahassee made her account brief. "I was called to the airport this afternoon, late. Jason sent for me. They had found something queer in one of the lockers there and wanted an identification. I—well, I thought the artifact looked a little like the rod of office in the Brooke Collection. So the head man—by the way," she turned now to Dr. Carey, "did you call that number he sent? He could have explained it all—"

"What number?" Dr. Joe looked puzzled.

"I told this Mr. Nye that Dr. Carey was coming to evaluate the Brooke Collection. He wrote a number on a card and asked for him to get in touch as soon as possible."

"Carey?" Dr. Joe turned his head.

The other showed no sign of discomfiture. "I did not know the man. If he wanted my services he need only approach me directly—which he did not. No, I did not call."

Why, wondered Tallahassee? The man seemed almost to take the suggestion as an insult.

"But you put this artifact in the safe?" Dr. Joe asked.

"Yes. It was in a lead-lined case—which is why Jason brought it up for me."

"Lead-lined?" Dr. Joe was plainly bewildered.

"They said that the artifact gave off some unidentified type of radiation. They were taking every precaution."

"It was African—a real artifact?"

"Look and see." Tallahassee, shaken as she had been by the sight of the office, now felt a rising irritation.

She put her hand to the safe dial, and then remembered the night alarms. But Dr. Joe had already anticipated her request and was on the phone to call Hawes and have those cut off. When the door opened, she brought out the case which was heavy enough that she needed both hands to swing it to the top of the desk. Flicking open the catch she lifted the cover. There the box lay as Dr. Joe went forward eagerly.

Tallahassee took the tongs at the top and lifted out the find with care. To her surprise, Dr. Carey did not join them by the desk. She glanced at him once and saw that he only sat there calmly, a faint, satirical smile on his thin lips, watching them as if they were edging into some trouble that he had no intention of warning them against. His attitude was stranger than ever, strange enough to awaken Tallahassee's feeling of something lurking here, waiting . . .

Dr. Joe had taken the tongs from her eagerly, was moving the box slowly around.

"Yes, yes! But, what? The style is a mixture—old, though, undoubtedly very old. And just left in a *locker!* We must run a test on it. Carey, what do you think it is— what culture?"

Dr. Carey got up. He moved swiftly, oddly. His eyes were now fastened avidly on the box and the malicious look was gone. With two strides he reached the desk, elbowing Tallahassee roughly to one side. Reaching forward before either of the other two could prevent it, for they were not prepared for his sudden move, he put one hand at either side of the box.

There was no sound, but when Dr. Carey lifted his hands, half the box came away. Inside was a small bundle wrapped in yellowed material.

"Don't!" Tallahassee caught at Carey's elbow. "The radiation!"

He did not even look at her. Instead he dropped the lid with a clatter to the desk and caught at the bundle. Dr. Joe attempted to snatch it away, his expression one of complete amazement.

Dr. Carey eluded him, just as he had jerked free from Tallahassee. He was tearing at the wrapping of the bundle frenziedly. The material peeled off in bits, as if the stuff had been weakened by age. What he held, after a second or two of fighting the covering, was an object about a foot long. And the shape was familiar to them all. This was an ankh—that very ancient key to all life which every representative of an Egyptian god or goddess carried in one hand. It had been carved of some crystalline-appearing substance and showed no fracture or erosion.

Dr. Carey dropped it to the desk top.

"What? Why?" He was wiping his hands up and down the front of his coat as if something he feared and hated clung to them. And now his face was pinched and drawn. "Why? . . ." he repeated in a voice higher than usual as if he needed an answer from them as to the reason for his actions.

At that moment there was a burst of thunder which seemed so close overhead that the roof itself might have been shattered. Tallahassee cowered and screamed, she could not help it. A second later the lights went out, and they stood in darkness.

"No! No! No!" Someone was crying out—the sound growing fainter with every denial.

"Dr. Joe." Somehow Tallahassee found her voice. "Dr.

Joe!" She tried to get around the table and ran into a chair, nearly losing her balance. Then she stood still.

There was light in the room. But it did not come from any bulb, any lamp she knew. It rayed out from the ankh on the table. The thing glowed.

And that glow drew her—just as she knew again that the presence she had sensed earlier was back, stronger than ever.

The ankh arose from the desk top. It was moving— and it was drawing her along after it. She tried to call out, to catch at the chair, at the wall, at anything that could serve as an anchorage. But there was nothing she could do.

"Dr. Joe!" This time her plea came as a faint whisper, the ability to say more had left her. That—that *presence* controlled her better than if someone had laid hands upon her shoulders and was pushing her ahead.

Frightened as she had never been before in her life, Tallahassee followed the floating, ghostly ankh one reluctant step at a time. They were in the outer hall now, she and the *thing* she could not see but well knew was with her, willing her to some task.

Here there was no light, either, but that given off by the ankh. However, it seemed to glow the brighter, so she could see the stairwell. Holding to the banister she went down and down, always that compulsion pushing her.

She found herself praying, not even in a whisper, because she could no longer voice even that much, but in her mind. This—this will that held her—it was a nightmare. This thing could not be happening—it could not! Yet it was.

They reached the fourth floor, the ankh swung into the hall there. Dimly, through her fear, Tallahassee realized where they were going—toward the three rooms that held the Brooke Collection. She had somehow surrendered part of herself. This *was* happening and apparently there was nothing she could do to prevent it.

"Tallahassee!"

Her name echoed hollowly from the stairwell behind. Dr. Joe! But he was too late—too late. . . . Too late for what, a part of her mind asked dully?

There was another roar of thunder but under it something else which pulsed even as the thunder died. Drums —the calling drums. Tallahassee forced her hands up over her ears, but she could not shut out that faint, demanding vibration of sound. And now there was added a tinkling, as if small bits of crystal were shaken one against another. That, too, she identified from a single moment of the past, the sistrum of the temple priestesses of old Egypt. They once had duplicated one in class and tried to use it as it must have been swung to summon the attention of the ancient gods.

She was going mad!

But she was not! Tallahassee's strong mind and intelligence began to rally. There was some logical explanation for all this. There must be! Part of her—that part which controlled her own movements—was in bondage to the influence of the presence. Her mind was still free.

They were at the door of the third and last room. Light greeted them. But not the normal light Tallahassee knew. This was a beam shooting from the depths of the main case in the room. She was not surprised at its source. The crystalline head of the rod of office held a fainter glow maybe, but one which matched, in part, that given off by the ankh floating ahead.

Then the ankh stopped, held in the air as if the girl herself supported it at the level of her breast. The compulsion changed. A new order had been given her, one she was no more able to resist than she had the unvoiced command that had brought her here.

Her hands moved out, willed by that other, to seek the

lock of the case. But it resisted her efforts. Now the compulsion strengthened, beat down upon her as physical blows might have done. The other will demanded that she free the rod. But she could not, it was locked. There was no way, no way at all. . . . The part of her mind that was free argued silently with the unseen, even as her body actually swayed back and forth under that beating command.

Out of the dark rang a voice. For one wild, hopeful moment Tallahassee thought either Dr. Joe or Hawes must have come to her rescue. Then she realized she could not understand a word of that impassioned speech. It was hot with anger, the emotion as strong as the will behind and about her. Yet it was not issuing from the presence that had brought her here.

A part of the control over her failed. As it withdrew, she somehow understood the rage that had gripped *it,* in turn, at the sound of that voice. But if it could reply it did not.

Now those words fell into the cadence of a strange chant, the rhythm of which was accented by a distant roll of drums. Tallahassee no longer wondered how she heard what she did, nor from whence it came. She only cowered before the display case in which the light-crowned rod lay, wanting to creep away from the site of battle. For the will that had brought her here was now facing another, and they were joined in struggle.

Tallahassee was suddenly caught up and hurled viciously against the case. She screamed, throwing her arms up over her face, fearing that the glass would shatter and cut her flesh to ribbons. But though she struck with bruising force, it was not enough to smash the case and accomplish the purpose of that will.

It withdrew, meshed again in a struggle with the invisible other.

More than one voice chanted now. She was sure of

that as she clung where the attack had left her, spread-eagled against the case. Her mind whirled. She felt sick with vertigo as forces beyond her knowledge or description stirred into a mad swirl about her. Then the ankh swung over her shoulder, hung directly above the case.

Wide-eyed, she watched the rod stir, rise until it stood vertical, without any support. It leaped upward, its glowing head thumped against the top of the case, while the ankh swooped downward to meet it at just the same point.

The glass cracked, shattered and fell. And the liberated rod spun through the air. Shadows gathered around it in a hectic dance, as it tipped, fell to the floor.

Above it, the ankh hovered as if trying to spur the staff to another effort. Was that the shadow of a *hand*— a hand so tenuous that it was only outlined in the glow of the ankh? It was something, of that Tallahassee was sure, and it was reaching for the rod. But before it settled close enough to grasp it, the rod itself shifted. Not upward again, but, snakelike for all its stiffness, across the floor.

Again the will seized upon Tallahassee, whirled her about, and gave her what amounted to a vicious shove after the slithering rod. The ankh flew up at her, as if to dash itself into her face and was warded off by what she could not see, so that it hovered, making effectual darts as she was forced to obey the orders of her strange captor. She must get the rod into her hands—that was the imperative now filling her whole mind.

Again a voice called out. And Tallahassee realized dimly that the chanting had ceased. The ankh swung away from her, skimmed through the air, to remain poised in one corner of the room toward which the rod was moving with Tallahassee stumbling after it. Since she moved puppetwise by the other will, she was clumsy, slow, trying always to break away from that hold.

But the will was implacable and its hate hot. Not that that hate was turned wholly against her, as a very inept tool it must make use of, but rather more at the enemy it fronted. She saw now that the rod lay quiet.

Once more, a ghostly outline moved across the glow at its head. Meanwhile the will hurled her forward. She tripped and fell as her outstretched hand closed on the other end of the rod just as it was plucked upward. Tallahassee held as she was commanded and forced to. Wraith-like that grasping hand might be—if hand it was —but there was strength in its hold upon the rod. The ankh dipped and touched the gleaming head of the staff.

It was like being caught in an explosion. There followed light, heat, pain, and such a noise as deafened Tallahassee. The girl had a terrifying sensation of being swung out over a vast void of nothingness. That other presence was left behind. Her hands were no longer glued to the rod by its command. But she kept her grasp for her very life's sake. In her welled the knowledge that, should she let go, the answer was death—a death that was unnatural enough to be worse than any her kind had feared since their first beginnings.

She centered every bit of the force and strength left in her to retain her hold. There was *nothing* around her, a nothingness so negative as to tear at her sanity. Hold— on!

Then the nothingness closed about her in a vast and horrible wrapping of utter blackness. Despairing, she lost consciousness.

IT was hot, as if she lay on the hearth of some furnace breathing in the stifling heat of the blast. Tallahassee tried to edge away from that heat, unaware as yet of anything else. She opened her eyes.

Sun—so blazing that it made an instant glare about her. With a little cry, Tallahassee shrank back, her hands over her eyes to shield them. It was hot, and she was lying under the sun—where? Her thoughts began to stir feebly, throwing off the torpor left from those last nightmare minutes.

Still shielding her eyes, she dug her elbows painfully against a hard surface on which she lay, levering up the forepart of her body, making herself look around.

Immediately before her was an outcrop of rock. And on its surface she could pick out a pattern deep-eroded by time into just faint lines. She crawled to that rock, lifting sand encrusted hands for its support in order to gain her feet. Then she turned, giddy and sick, feeling

as if each labored movement might send her sailing out
again into that dark void. Her dulled mind jibbed at
even thinking of that—place.

More rocks beyond. Or were those long-ago quarried
stones built into a piece of tumbled wall? But at their
foot. . . .

Tallahassee stifled the scream in her throat, made herself blink, and blink again, to be sure she really saw that
body stretched out on rock and sand.

The stranger lay face down, arms flung out above the
head. In one hand was grasped the ankh, in the other the
rod. They no longer pulsed with light. Or perhaps, in this
blinding sunlight, their auras of radiation could not be
distinguished.

Tallahassee inched along the rock which was her support. Was the stranger unconscious? And who—and what
—and where? . . . She felt as if she were going mad, or
had passed the border of sanity during the time that the
rod had drawn her on.

There was a thin, almost gossamer cotton robe on the
body, so finely woven that one could see the gleam of
darker flesh through it. It was simply made, reaching
from armpit to ankle, with two broad straps of the same
material holding it over the shoulders, a belt which gave
off glints of gemlike color against the dead white of the
garment. The stranger's shoulder-length hair had been
woven into many tiny braids, each tipped with a bead of
gold, and there was another band of the same precious
metal forming a narrow diadem to hold those braids in
confinement.

Tallahassee was reminded of something. She moved a
fraction closer, fearing to stoop lest her present vertigo
send her toppling against the stranger. Instead she
dropped carefully to her knees and put out a hand to the
shoulder where the brown skin was a shade or so darker
than her own.

With an effort she rolled the stranger over, the body limply slack in her hold. She was sure somehow that this was death. But, as the other's face came into view, Tallahassee screamed and flinched away.

Sand was matted on the generous lips, caught in eyebrows that had been darkened and extended by the use of a heavy cosmetic. But the face itself—NO!

Save for the slight difference in the color of their skins, she was looking down at the same features she saw every time she stood before a mirror! Oh there were differences—the brows artificially lengthened toward the temples and darkened, thick lines drawn under the now-closed eyes, while the headband rose in front to the likeness of a striking serpent.

"Egypt—" Tallahassee whispered. "Egypt and royal . . ." For that serpent diadem could be worn only by a woman of the Blood, and one placed very close to the throne itself.

She scuttled back on her hands and knees. The girl was dead, she was certain of that. Now she looked around wildly . . . .

They were in a place where sand had been scoured away, perhaps by the wind of some dune-lashing storm, perhaps by human effort. There were ruins all about, stones pitted and defaced by those same grit-filled winds. And she was nowhere on the earth she knew! Shaking with a growing fear, she crouched against the rock that had earlier supported her and tried to understand what had happened. There was no sane explanation for this, none at all!

She was still locked in rising panic when she caught sounds, first faint and then growing louder. It was such chanting as she had heard just before this unbelievable thing had happened to her. Only now it rang far more clear and distinct. It—they—were coming! She tried to force herself once more to her feet, but she literally did not have the strength to move. She could only huddle where she was as the nightmare went on and on.

There was no word in that rise of sound which she could understand. But she began to believe she could detect more than a single voice. Once more Tallahassee made a desperate effort. She must hide! Only, under this blistering sun, in this waste of stone and sand, there was no place of concealment she could see.

The voices ceased suddenly. Now came the ringing of a sistrum. Tallahassee gave a weak laugh. Egypt! But why was her unconscious (which certainly must be directing this weird dream) so set on reproducing Egypt?

And she was so hot, thirsty. Perhaps back in her own world she was burning with a fever. Or—a scrap of memory flipped through her thoughts—did radiation, an overdose of the strange radiation from the ankh, lie at the bottom of this?

She heard a sharp cry and turned her head. The figure coming between the broken bits of walls was all of a piece with the rest. A woman, who from Tallahassee's present squatting position, looked supernaturally tall, was running toward them. Her figure, covered by the same kind of white dress as the dead girl wore, was human and female.

Only, on her shoulders instead of a human head, rested the golden head of a lioness wearing a diadem of two metal feathers, spine to spine, standing tall and straight from the top of the lioness's rounded skull.

The creature sped toward the sprawled body of the girl. Then she caught sight of Tallahassee for the first time and stopped almost in mid-stride. There was no change of expression on the set features of the golden beast-face. But, though the lips did not move, there came a series of words which held the inflection of a question.

Tallahassee slowly shook her head. As the lioness head faced her more closely she could see now that it was a mask, for the eyes were holes through which the wearer must look. Swiftly, the other turned from Tallahassee to the dead girl. She knelt by the body, her masked head moving slowly back and forth, looking first at the painted face against the sand and then to Tallahassee. Almost reluctantly she put out her hand and picked up the ankh. But the rod she left lying where the dead had dropped it.

Twice she stretched out her hand tentatively as if to grasp it but did not complete the motion. Then— Tallahassee started—there came a gust of wind so cold that in this sun-soaked place it was like a blow. The woman arose, faced in the direction from which that wind blew. Tallahassee saw a strange movement in the air, as if some shadowy thing whirled about and about.

The lioness-masked woman swung up the ankh. From behind her mask came a series of explosive words carrying with them the force of a curse. With the ankh she swiftly drew a series of crosses back and forth in the air as if so erecting a wall of defense against whatever struggled there to come to them.

A feeble thrust of the will that had held Tallahassee and made her obey strove again to enter her mind. However, this time she could stand firm. Far off—very faintly —did she then hear an angry cry? She was not sure.

But the movement of the air grew less, vanished. The woman waited for a long moment, the eyes of the mask turned to the place where the disturbance had been. Then Tallahassee saw the rigid tenseness of her body relax. Whatever had striven to reach them had failed.

Now the mask swung once more in Tallahassee's direction and she who wore it made a sharp, commanding gesture.

Though she did not want to, Tallahassee crawled away from her rock and reached for the rod, obeying that deftly signed order. Once more her fingers clutched at its smooth surface and she raised it upright. The masked one stood as still as might the image of some goddess in an ancient temple.

Then once more her voice broke the heated air. At her peremptory call, two more women came running lightly into view. Both were dressed in the same plain white garments, their hair braided into the same design favored by the dead girl, squared off at the shoulders, their eyes rimmed and lengthened by strokes of black. But the headdresses they wore were bands of material, each centered over the forehead by a medallion of gold worked into the likeness of a lioness, matching the mask of their superior.

They showed signs of shock and excitement at what they found. But at the sharp-voiced command of their leader they gathered up the body of the dead. Tallahassee was beckoned to follow them.

In the heat, her long skirt and blouse clung stickily to her skin as she tottered along with the women, mainly because she could see nothing else to do. Where was she? How she had come here? She felt that she must force all save the immediate present to the back of her mind or she would become insane.

The bleak ruins were, she discovered as she rounded the largest rock where she had taken refuge, on the edge of a slope. There were outcrops of parts ·of walls, a series of small, sharp-pointed pyramids, the caps of many of them missing, a dry dead land going down to a single large and pillared building which appeared to be in some state of repair.

But it was the sight of those small pyramids that drew a gasp from Tallahassee. She could close her eyes and mind-picture a series of photographs she knew very well, indeed.

Not Egypt, but its darker, lesser sister—Meroë of the Nubians. Meroë where had gathered the last, faded remnants of the glory of old Egypt, which had indeed provided, at a later time, three Pharaohs to conquer northward, to rule the whole of the near-extinguished land of ancient Khem and become wearers of the proud double crown. Meroë about which so little was known, so many guesses made. Was it Meroë that lay now before her? But how—how had she come *here?*

The two women she followed carried their burden toward that single great building. Tallahassee did not turn her head to see, but she was well aware that behind her stalked the lioness-priestess—for priestess she must be.

Meroë had worshipped a lion god—Apedemek. There had been no lioness, unless one remembered Shekmet, the war goddess, of the more northern lands.

Again she moved under a measure of compulsion, though it was not as great as that which had sent her through the museum corridors. She might even challenge it if she wished, Tallahassee believed. But to what purpose? It was far better to keep with these until she could somehow discover what had happened. The rod of office slipped in her sweaty hand, she took a firmer grip upon it. Why had the priestess given it to her? It must be highly important to these people, whoever they might be, yet she had been ordered to carry it. Tallahassee could only believe that they were afraid of it in some manner. If it *was* what had brought her here—then she could understand that. On the other hand, *if* that was the truth, then it might just be a way of breaking this strange dream and returning to her own time and world. Thus the closer she kept to it now the better.

They passed from the glare of the sun and its draining heat into the temple. Fronting them was Apedemek himself wearing the double crown, in one hand the symbolic plow of the kings and queens of Meroë. The stone face was very old, eroded, but there was majesty in it—an aura of confident power that was not quite arrogance.

At the feet of the ten-foot statue the women laid down the body of the girl, smoothing her robe about her slender legs, crossing her hands to lie palms down and open on her motionless breast. Then one of them knelt at her head and one at her feet and began to wail.

Another sharp command from the priestess silenced them. She motioned Tallahassee to go on, past Apedemek, into an inner room of the temple. Here were signs of occupancy—though Tallahassee thought this was only temporary. Four thick rolls of padding might form beds at night, and there were cushions covered with brightly patterned material on the strips of matting that cloaked the floor. Baskets and two tall jars occupied one corner. But what was opposite those, across the room, brought Tallahassee's instant attention. Three plates of metal glistening black, over which played a sheen of faint rainbow colors, formed a small, flat-topped pyramid. Set upright on that was an object which certainly had no place among the signs of ancient past which lay all about.

It was an oblong of glass and yet opaque, milk-white. Up and down the three surfaces she could see, ran a ripple of ever-changing color, to outshine the rainbows on the stand. The oblong was perhaps two feet in height, and from it came a soft hum that Tallahassee could only associate with smooth-running machinery. But this was so anachronistic in comparison with all about it, she could only stare and wonder.

She had come into the room obeying the priestess's gestures. But none of the others followed her. Instead the priestess laid the ankh carefully on the threshold and raised her masked head, making a firm sign that Tallahassee was to remain where she was. Then she stepped back into the main portion of the temple.

The girl made a circuit of the chamber. She discovered that the tall jars in the corner were covered, and when she slipped the lid off the nearest she could see water in it. Instantly, as if the sight of the liquid had triggered her response, she was so thirsty that she longed to raise the whole jar and let its contents take the taste of sand grit from her. There was a cup resting on a pile of plates nearby and she seized that.

The drinking of that water more than anything else roused her out of the bewilderment that had held her since she had awakened among the ruins. She did not remember ever drinking or eating (for now she had reached for a date lying with others in a sticky little pool on a plate, above which was a transparent cover easy enough to lift) in any dream before.

The date was very sticky, for it must have been steeped in honey. Too sweet, she had to wash the taste of it from her mouth with another gulp of lukewarm water. Food, water, the mats to sleep on—and that thing in the corner which certainly was *not* of Meroë, nor of Egypt either.

The steady hum it had emitted vanished in a flash of brighter light that rose, not in random lines now, but in a well-marked spiral on the front panel. At the same time, there came a crackle of sound that grew louder and more insistent with every second.

Tallahassee approached the thing carefully. It was eerie, mainly because it was alien to all the rest in this room, all that she had seen outside, enough so to make one wary. However, as quickly as it had appeared, the brilliant spiral of light vanished, leaving again only the vibrant hum.

There was only one door to the room, but high on the walls some stones had fallen out, so that the sun made bright, light patches here and there. Tallahassee, oddly reluctant to turn her back on the pillar thing, crept softly to the door. She had no idea of the plan of this temple. And now, from what must be the outer shrine, she heard once more the tinkle of the sistrum, a murmur of voices chanting in a tone hardly above a whisper.

Could she slip out? Tallahassee studied the ankh lying in the doorway. It was enough in the shadows to show once again a small shimmer of radiance about it. When she tried to edge past, it was like meeting a solid surface —not hard and stationary, like a wall, but a barrier that gave a little and then repelled.

Retreating to one of the cushions on the floor, the girl sat cross-legged and tried to assess her position. Now she deliberately did what she had kept herself from doing earlier, attempted to trace this unbelievable situation back to the very beginning.

She had indeed been forced along after the ankh to the room of the Brooke Collection. There had been a seeming confrontation there between two invisible wills—perhaps personalities. Then had followed her own compulsion to capture the rod, her full awakening in the sand and ruins.

This was all too vividly real and had lasted far too long to be just a dream. She was not and had never been into drugs. But perhaps this was the sort of thing a user might imagine when high.

The evidences of the past, she knew, could be drawn from her own memory. Only, to refute that, there was that thing in the corner which was plainly not of any Meroë she knew through her studies. If she was not drugged, nor dreaming—what had happened to her? And why did the dead girl have Tallahassee's own features, features which could not be disguised even by the exotic eye makeup, the difference in skin shade?

Where *was* she?

There was no logical, nor acceptable answer for what had happened: none that she could muster anyway.

It was hot, so hot, in spite of the thick walls of masonry. A flicker on the wall caught her eye. A lizard ran swiftly into nowhere before she had more than glimpsed it. She could hear a shuffling sound and watched the doorway, alerted, as the priestess entered, having stooped to pick up the ankh which so efficiently had locked in her captive.

One of the other women came behind her and, paying no attention to Tallahassee, went directly to a woven basket with a lid. This she raised. Through the dead air of the place, Tallahassee caught a spicy scent as the woman shook out a white robe similar to those they all wore. She laid it to one side and stooped to dip once more into the basket, this time to come up with a pair of sandals having thongs to slide between great toes and the rest, ties to lash about the ankles. Last of all she brought out a stand on which was a wig, the hair of which had been arranged in the many small gold-tipped braids such as the dead girl had worn. On this she carefully fitted what the priestess now handed her—the circlet bearing the striking snake.

Having overseen the assembling of this wardrobe, the priestess now turned to Tallahassee, making unmistakable gestures for her to shed her present clothing. When the girl did not comply the priestess raised the ankh, her threat plain. If Tallahassee did not obey of her free will, the forces the priestess could employ would be called upon.

Slowly Tallahassee did as commanded. As she let fall her last garment, she found that the lesser priestess was beside her carrying a small pot. Using some greasy but spicy substance from that container, she began to smear it, with even strokes, over Tallahassee's arms and shoulders.

She worked quickly and expertly. And, when she had done, Tallahassee saw that her skin had been completely matched to the shade of the women with her. She was helped into the shift dress: a gemmed girdle, which she was sure she had seen on the dead girl, was hooked about her. Then they motioned her to kneel and the lesser priestess hacked at Tallahassee's hair with a knife, shearing it closer to the skull.

Her eyes were encircled by brush strokes from another cosmetic pot. And, at last, the wig bearing the diadem was carefully fitted on. The lesser priestess drew back as the masked one surveyed the result of her labors —critically, Tallahassee guessed. She did not doubt that she was being deliberately disguised to take the place of the dead.

Once more the bewilderment receded. This time she felt a small excitement rising in her. Dream, hallucination, no matter what this was—her curiosity was now firmly engaged. Meroë's fragmentary history had always interested her. Now she wanted to know how long her illusion was going to last, how far it would take her. Oddly enough, she wanted, somehow, to go along with the play (for play it seemed to her to be), as long as she could.

When she stood once more, the rod (which none had touched, but which the priestess had gestured her to take up again) in her hand, she longed to know what kind of an appearance she made. The priestess stood very still. Tallahassee could not see the eyes behind the mask holes, but she did not doubt they were now sweeping her from head to foot, an inspection that was broken only when there came a loud crackle from the lighted block in the corner.

She saw the priestess start as if in amazement. Then she hurried over, to drop to her knees before that column of spiralling color which filled the front panel. That she listened to something which made sense to her, Tallahassee guessed. There came a hastily smothered gasp from the other woman who sped to the door and was gone.

Tallahassee's curiosity rose like a fever. If she only understood, could really *know* what all this meant!

The crackle stopped. However, now the priestess reached forth her hand and made a sweeping, wiping motion across the block. The spiral vanished. What formed in its turn was a symbol Tallahassee knew, the Eye of Horus. As it held there steady, the priestess brought back her mask even closer to the surface of the block and spoke—in soft, sputtery sounds Tallahassee thought were not the same used in the chanting she had earlier heard.

The eye blinked out of sight. Once more there was only a loose play of unformed color, the hum of the machine. The priestess arose to approach Tallahassee. At this short distance, the girl could well see the dark human irises within the eye pits of the mask. She felt the other's pressing need for communication though how she realized that was what the other wanted, she could not have said.

"What do you want of me?" Tallahassee asked.

The other pointed to the doorway and then to herself and to Tallahassee. From the heavy front panel of her girdle she drew a long knife and aimed it first toward her own breast and then toward Tallahassee, again pointing to the doorway when she had done—this time with an almost vicious thrust through the air itself.

The girl made a guess she believed was not too wild. "Danger—for us both," she said aloud.

Once more, those eyes surveyed her steadily and searchingly. Then the lioness mask nodded only a fraction, as if to do more might send the whole thing spinning from its wearer's head.

The priestess pointed from her knife to the rod, and then to the knife again. Was she trying to say that the rod was as much of a weapon as the blade she had drawn, Tallahassee wondered. But a weapon to be used against what—or whom?

Her own head jerked as she heard a sound overhead—a sound that grew louder and louder. Again it was familiar in part, though not in any world where Meroë ruled. Unless Tallahassee was completely mistaken that was an aircraft of some sort, and it sounded as if it were coming in for a landing!

$\mathcal{T}$HE priestess made no move, save to turn her head slightly toward the door, as if all her attention was given to what might be happening without. After what seemed only seconds, Tallahassee heard the voices of men, raised in anger, she believed. Now the priestess stepped forward beside Tallahassee, so they were ranged together facing the door.

There came a sharp crack, enough to make Tallahassee start. She could not be sure, but that had sounded very much like a shot! Like the lighted block in the corner, the thought of modern weapons here was anachronistic. Fingers touched her arm. The priestess made a small gesture, one that urged Tallahassee to raise the rod before her. She remembered of old the common stance of most of the Egyptian statues, ankh, flail, crook so upheld.

The other women backed into the room, their voices raised in hot protest. Herding them so came three men.

Seeing them, the belief she had somehow returned to

47

the ancient past vanished for Tallahassee. By rights these newcomers should have worn kilts, carried spears or bows. Instead, the newcomers were closer to her own world in their dress, for each wore a one-piece uniform, cut off at elbows and knees.

The garment was a dull green in color, relieved only by a mask of Apedemek on the shoulder. Incongruously, their headgear, striped in two shades of green, did resemble the ancient sphinx headdress of the Egyptian fighting man. For the rest, they each carried what was manifestly a weapon, like and yet unlike, Tallahassee believed, the guns of her time. These were neither rifle nor handgun, but between those two in length. And the short barrels pointed along their own forearms, as they held them ready to fire.

On catching sight of Tallahassee they halted—their eyes went wide. Shock or mere surprise? She could not be sure. The priestess beside her broke into speech. Never had Tallahassee longed so much to know what was going on than at this moment.

The two men behind the leader took a couple of steps backward, their discomfiture plain to read. What or who they had expected to find here, it was not those they fronted now. The priestess raised her ankh and spoke commandingly, while the leader of the trio scowled at her. A scar, which split his right cheek from temple to chin, did not add to any suggestion of mercy in his expression. He gave no ground, only glowered at the lioness-masked woman.

The rod! Tallahassee decided to try a small experiment. She held the staff a little aslant so that its top crystal now inclined toward the man. He quickly shifted gaze from the priestess to the girl. She saw the change in his eyes.

He was afraid! Afraid of either her or the rod, and she believed it the latter. Now an expression of sullen defeat warped his scarred features. Tallahassee took one step forward and then another. He retreated, but not as fast as his two followers, who broke and ran as the girl approached them.

Their leader was not giving in easily. Tallahassee sensed danger building in this man. She had always been able somehow to pick up emotional reactions of others to herself, knowing when she was accepted, tolerated, or disliked. But it was no dislike this man radiated, rather it was hate. She was as certain of that as if he had shouted curses in her face.

Driving him this way might be the worst move she could make. Yet the two women stepped quickly aside, and she was aware that the priestess walked steadily behind her. They *wanted* her to do just as she was doing!

The soldier growled under his breath, a hostile mutter, yet he backed step by slow step, as she advanced. Now they passed into the outer chamber of the temple with the statue of Apedemek looming behind the man's shoulder. Back and back again—outside into the white blare of the desert sun, the furnace heat.

She caught a glimpse of something standing not too far away. But she could not look at it closely. It was necessary instead to keep her eyes on the man before her. Back still more until they were at the very edge of the temple pavement. Suddenly he swung his weapon by its strap up across his shoulder and spoke a last sharp sentence in which she could read menace without understanding the words.

He seemed reluctant to turn his back on her. His withdrawal was rather crablike, glancing at her with a side look as he descended the wide outer steps and stalked away—his whole body expressing his angry impotence— to a flyer.

To Tallahassee's eyes that vehicle possessed some of the attributes of a helicopter, save there were no whirling blades on top. Rather, once the man had made his way to the opening in its side and climbed within, it arose in a cloud of grit and sand by a method she did not understand.

There had been an insignia painted on the flyer's side but those markings had no meaning for the girl. Again a touch on her wrist, and the priestess made that small inclination of her masked head, suggesting their return to the interior of the temple ruin. One of the women behind spoke and then spat outward in the direction of the vanished flyer. The roar of its withdrawal was already fading.

The priestess wasted no more time. Instead she moved at a pace that closely approached a run, Tallahassee hurrying after, to reach the inner chamber. There the masked woman, once more on her knees before the lighted block, spoke to it with an imperative burst of words.

Tallahassee moved closer to the woman who had spat after the retreating soldiers.

"Who?" She tried to get into that word of her own language the sound of inquiry as she pointed to the outside.

For a moment it would seem that the woman was not going to answer, if indeed she understood Tallahassee's query. Then she spoke slowly and deliberately one word:

"Userkof." At least it sounded like that.

The part of Tallahassee's knowledge that had already found the small, disturbing, familiar hints in this place seized upon the sound. Userkof—Nubian of the past—or Egyptian? She was sure it was a man's name. But was it that of the leading intruder, or of one who had sent him? If she only *knew*. Her ignorance made her want to hurl the rod at the wall and then do a little therapeutic screaming. *When* would she ever find out what had happened, where she was, and why? The "why" might out-weigh all the other points, she suspected.

They had made her up to play a part. Apparently, she was someone who, with the rod in hand, had authority to banish armed men who had certainly not come here for anything but trouble. And she had only a single name——Userkof—on which to build an answer.

Names? Names were important. Among some people the personal name held such great importance that they never revealed it to strangers, lest that give another some psychic hold over them. She could begin with names—the first stumbling exchange in any language.

With her thumb she energetically thumped her own breast and asked again:

"Who?"

The woman glanced first at the priestess still busy crooning to the slab. This time her hesitation was even more marked. Yet she answered at last:

"Ashake."

"Ashake," Tallahassee repeated, striving to give the word the same pronunciation. Now she indicated the priestess:

"Who?"

"Jayta." This time the pause was not long. Perhaps the woman found that, since the sky had not fallen the first time, she dared be more helpful.

"Jayta." Now the girl's finger pointed to the woman. "Who?"

"Makeda."

The other woman was identified as Idia. Tallahassee was faintly encouraged. If they just cooperated a little, she might be able to find out something.

"Where?" She moved her hand about in a gesture that she hoped would be intelligible to the other, who watched her very closely. But the three words she then got in answer meant nothing at all. And it was hard to be baffled again just when she had made progress, no matter how small.

The priestess arose from before the slab and uttered what could only be a string of orders. Both the other women hurried to draw together the pallets on the floor, pile them in a corner. They paid no attention to anything else but the basket from which they had taken the clothes Tallahassee now wore. That they carried out into the shadow of Apedemek's statue.

Jayta was busy with the slab, pressing her fingers carefully about the lowest of the three square blocks on which it was positioned. As if that had released some mounting, she picked it up and the light now vanished from its surface. An inclination of her head sent Tallahassee before her. It was plain they were making preparations to leave the temple. Leaving for where?

If she could only see more than just the priestess's eyes through the mask. One could learn much from an expression if one was attentive.

But she tried once more, waving her hand toward the outside and asking:

"Where?"

Again came more than one word, and those meant nothing at all. Yet Tallahassee believed that they were not the same Makeda had uttered earlier. Their destination? And how were they to travel?

That was answered soon enough by a second roar from the air. The invaders back with new forces? Tallahassee took a closer grip on the rod. A second party might not be so easily cowed.

Once more a flyer set down, spinning sand and grit in a murky cloud, wide enough to hide the whole entrance to the temple. As that settled, figures dropped from the machine, came trotting toward them. Uniforms again, but not the dull green of the first party. These were of a red shade, close to rust. And those wearing them were unmistakably women.

At the sight of Tallahassee, three of them dropped to their knees and raised one hand palm out, but with the other hand held ready the same type of weapon the men had borne. Their leader did not kneel, merely raised one hand to Tallahassee, and then broke into a spate of excited speech.

The priestess made a sharp answer, waved them on toward the waiting flyer. Tallahassee went with a faint reluctance. She had come into this world at this point. If she left here—was there any way she could find her way back to her own place? For she was convinced now, in spite of herself, that this could not be a dream. And she had no reason to think she was hallucinating, unless the unknown radiation given off by the ankh had induced it.

Within the flyer, quarters were somewhat cramped. The priestess and Tallahassee were given a double seat while the temple women and the Amazons settled down on the flooring, drawing webbing belts over them. Tallahassee could see another uniformed woman at the controls. She was given little time to examine her surroundings before the flyer lifted with a jerk that made her feel unpleasantly like being caught in a runaway elevator.

She was not next to the small window, so could not catch any glimpse of the terrain over which they flew. But she had a sensation of speed which was surely greater than that of the helicopters of her own world.

This situation was like facing a giant puzzle, or rather two puzzles, where all pieces had been arbitrarily mixed so that one could make no sense out of either. The masked priestess, the ruins—those she could better accept somehow than a flyer. She had seen the like of the former throughout the years of her study, if only in pictures. But what had ancient Egypt or Nubia to do with unfamiliar weapons and vehicles?

Her head ached under the weight of the wig they had forced on her. She longed to jerk it off, yet somehow knew that even so small an act of independence might bring serious consequences. The leader of the soldiers opened a small compartment set against the wall of the pilot's cubby and brought out a metal flask and some handleless cups. In spite of the unsteadiness of the flyer she poured a measure of liquid into a cup, about half-full, and handed it carefully to the priestess, who, in turn, with a show of ceremony, held it out to Tallahassee.

She accepted with a murmur of thanks and drank. The contents was tart, and so cold that she had a momentary shock. She drank thirstily, realizing again that her body needed this though she had not been aware of that until she drank.

Another cup was offered to the priestess, but she declined. Tallahassee began to wonder how the woman could endure wearing the mask so continually, and why she did so. At the temple it might have been for some reasons of ceremony, but why did she cling to it now?

Then abruptly, they spiraled earthward, to set down with a slight jar. The Amazon officer made haste to open the door, scramble out, with her three followers, as if expecting some trouble against which they must guard. Jayta, if Jayta the priestess really was, touched Talla-hassee gently on the arm and signed for her to go next.

She moved rather awkwardly, for though the priestess matched her in height as did the leader of the soldiers, the others were at least four or five inches shorter and the flyer had manifestly been designed to their norm instead of hers. As the girl came into the open down the single step, she was no longer in the desert. The sere stone and sand, the blank walls of the ruins were gone.

Here was a lush green that rested her eyes. A few feet away a path of stones set in colorful mosaic patterns led into a tunnel walled by palm trees and brilliantly flowered bushes. She sniffed the perfume of flowers, heavy, almost cloying to the senses, saw bits of what could only be a building of at least three stories engulfed by the lush greenery.

The Amazons stood at stiff attention, two on either side. As Tallahassee moved slowly and hesitantly down the walk, they fell in behind, leaving only the priestess a step or two to the rear as they went.

This was going it blind all right. She did not have the least idea of where she was heading, or what she was to do here. But it was a vast relief to get into the shadow of the palms and the tall branches of the bushes. There was a flash along the path toward her and Tallahassee froze, then gave a small laugh of embarrassment. For the newcomers were two kittens. Very superior kittens, since each had a gold ring in the right ear near the tip and wore in addition a collar with small tinkling bells.

The kittens halted, their baby heads up at an angle, watching her with that unblinking stare that cats use to make humans uneasy. If they were the dead girl's cats— then the imposture Tallahassee had been ordered to . . . . She stooped and held out her hand. All depended now on them. Suppose they unmasked her as a stranger, what would the Amazons behind her do? If Ashake were a princess, as the diadem on her stifling wig signified— well, what might be the penalty for impersonating her? The larger of the kittens advanced hesitantly to sniff at Tallahassee's fingers. Sniffed a second time, then made a quick dab with a rough little tongue tip against her flesh.

The young cat uttered a sound which was not quite a mew and bounded at its companion. With a cuff of a paw it passed, streaking once more down the walk, its brother or sister now in wild pursuit.

Tallahassee gave a sigh of relief she hoped was not audible. She did not ask about her role, but she certainly wanted to be sure that she was not going to be unmasked at a time most dangerous to her.

Jayta spoke, addressing Tallahassee with deference she had not paid before. She gestured to the building only half seen among the thick growth, plainly urging the girl on.

They passed through a thicker growth which appeared to mark a hedge between a garden and the landing field. Now the building before them showed clearly above the carefully tended flower beds. Massive pillars flanked the front, supporting an overhang of the roof. And the pillars, like the ruins, were familiar. These were not the columns the western world had inherited from the Greeks. Rather they were designed to resemble thick stalks of flowers, formalized half-open buds forming their crowns.

The door they guarded was very wide, and gave, not on a hallway or room, but rather on an inner court, the center of which was occupied by a long pool in which living lotus plants fringed the sides. Guards by the door snapped to attention, Amazons again. Beyond, waited a group of white-clad women who scattered at an order from the priestess, though they went reluctantly, many looking at Tallahassee as if they expected her to countermand Jayta. A second order sent the two women who had come with them from the temple, to one side and ahead, carrying between them the dress basket.

As those two passed through one of the doors that lined the four sides of the inner court, Tallahassee caught the hint. Clever of Jayta—she now knew just where she was to go and would make no betraying slip in choosing her room. As an embroidered door hanging fell behind her she looked curiously about these new quarters.

The walls were painted with a stylized pattern of lotus blossoms, bordering the head of a lioness which matched the mask her companion wore. Here was a narrow bed, the four legs of which had been inlaid to suggest a leopard's legs and paws. Folding tables stood beside two straight-backed, feline-footed chairs. And there was a padded bench before a more massive piece of furniture which consisted of two sets of drawers, an open space between, topped by a slab of inlaid wood on which stood a mirror, together with a number of small and fancifully carved and inlaid boxes and pots. As Tallahassee came a step or so farther into the chamber she caught full sight of herself in the mirror and gasped.

She faced a stranger. The thick makeup about her eyes—the lines of which extended well back to the edge of the wig—were almost as concealing as a mask. Her darker skin, the wig itself—she might have walked out from some painted tomb wall in Thebes or Memphis!

"Ashake!" She was not aware she had said that name aloud until she heard herself.

It was hard to turn away from that stranger on the mirrored surface. She—she was *not* Ashake. Suddenly her hands began to shake. She might even have dropped the rod had not a quick exclamation of warning made her look away from that deceiving reflection.

One of the temple women approached bearing a long case covered with gold, in raised design upon it those same spirit-protecting medallions she had pointed out on the box—where, how long ago? The priestess pressed fingers at two places to lift the lid. Inside, a soft cushioning carried an impression, a hollow long and narrow, meant undoubtedly to contain the rod. Thankfully Tallahassee fitted that within and saw the box shut and laid upon the bed.

Then Jayta's hands went to the back of her own head, pressed at the nape of her neck much as she had on the case for the rod. A moment later the mask fell into two parts which one of the women took from her.

Tallahassee found herself facing a woman who had no claim to beauty. Her nose was a hawk's proud beak, her

chin pointed and seeming (when seen in profile) to curve
up to meet that same beak. The hair, close-cropped to
her skull, was silvered, and she wore no makeup to en-
large her eyes or to give more color to her full lips. It
was the face of one who had her orders obeyed and
swiftly. Yet the strength in it, Tallahassee thought, was
not marred by any touch of cruelty. Had she, in her own
mind, ever built up an idea of justice personified, the
answer could have come close to Jayta.

Now the priestess studied Tallahassee closely in turn,
even as an artist might minutely examine some product
of his hands, searching ruthlessly for the slightest fault.
The other women retreated to the door, raised their
hands in salute, and were gone. Tallahassee drew a deep
breath and allowed herself to sit on one of the two chairs.
Jayta continued to stand until Tallahassee, guessing at
the cause, waved her companion to the other. Though
this room was infinitely cooler than the ruined temple,
she wanted to throw off the wig, rid herself of the grit
that clung to her stained skin. Yet now she needed communication most.

There was a movement by the door and Idia slipped in
again, almost furtively. She held a covered basket in her
hands which she offered to Jayta. What the priestess
lifted out was a box from which dangled two cords. Idia
hurriedly pushed one of the tables closer and Jayta settled the box on that. She picked up one of the cords and
inserted the hard tip of it in her ear, signaling for Tallahassee to do the same with the other.

The girl nearly jerked free again when she felt the
result. Telepathy? No, for this exchange apparently
needed the box. But she had indeed received a message—
not from lip to ear, but mind to mind.

"Do not fear, Lady."

Tallahassee half lifted her hand to pull out the cord,

then forced her nerves under better control. This was what she wanted most: communication—explanation.

"Who are you? Where am I? How did I get here?" She asked her questions in a quick whisper.

"Do not speak—not until you know our tongue, Lady. There are far too many shadows who have ears and mouths to whisper in the wrong places what those ears have picked up. I am the Daughter-of-Apedemek, though many of our people have regretfully turned aside from the True Learning in these years. As to where you are—that I cannot say more than this is the Empire of Amun in the two thousandth year since the parting of North and South. It is not your world. As to how you got here—now that is a tale which must be made short for we have so little time. But it follows this pattern as a cub follows its dam.

"What lies there"—she gestured to the now encased rod—"is the soul of our nation. Oh,"—she made a grimace as if she had bitten upon something very sour—"there are many nowadays who do not believe in the teachings that made Amun great under our Lord, the Sun. They lean upon the work of their own hands, say that what is born of their thoughts is theirs only and comes not from the teaching of One greater than themselves. Yet even those loose thinkers know that without the Rod in her hands no order the Candace gives will be obeyed. Without it she is nothing, for in the Rod is all the strength of her Blood. And only one of the Blood may hold it."

"Candace!" Tallahassee forgot the other's warning. "That was the title of the ancient Queens of Meroë!"

The eyes turned toward her, narrowed. "Who are you who speak of the Place of the Dead?" The demand was like a pain in her head, sharp enough to bring her hand up to her forehead. And there was a note of hostility in it. . . .

TALLAHASSEE hesitated. *Where* she was became more the question she wanted answered. "Empire
of Amun" meant nothing. Yet Jayta obviously reacted
quickly to the mention of Meroë. Now she tried to frame
her counter question with care.

"I do not know the Empire of Amun." She made her
admission first. "To my knowledge very long ago—
perhaps two thousand years—there was a kingdom of
Meroë whose people held even Egypt for a short space.
But that was swept away long ago, leaving only ruins
and a few names of kings and queens of whom we know
little else than those names, today. So—I ask you—of
your charity, Daughter-of-Apedemek, where am I now?"

Now it was Jayta's turn to wait for a moment which
stretched even longer for Tallahassee. She thought out
her reply slowly at last:

"I do not know how much knowledge you may have
of what can be done by the ancient powers. It is only

within my own lifetime that certain of us who are trained to the Far Sight and the Command of the Upper Way have come to be sure of what I tell you now. And if you need proof that we speak the truth take your own presence here for that.

"We have ceaselessly through centuries wrought with certain mind skills that are very old. You spoke of Egypt —do you mean the Land of Khem, of the Two Crowns?"

Tallahassee nodded.

"Ah, then you must also know that those of the Inner Teaching there, too, had talents beyond those of ordinary men. When the invaders broke Khem, these initiates, together with some of the Blood, fled southward, coming into Kush where even the Men of the Bow recognized them for what they were and gave them refuge. More and more they strove to set their learning to the use of the Inner Ways. Then Kush itself in time was assaulted—by the new barbarians in the north, by the greedy traders of Axum who would reduce our power to naught and gather into their hands all the wealth that flowed through Meroë.

"Again must a core of the Learned and those of the Blood flee—this time west, into a land that had never been linked with Khem and where they were strangers, indeed. But in those days they had harvested enough from their experiments to give them the power to win rulership over the natives of that land who were unenlightened and took the Talent for a magic they could not themselves command.

"It continued a long time, this searching for knowledge. And there were years when our rulership was disputed, sometimes when only a scarce handful of us held the secrets we had been so long in winning. Around us the world changed, sometimes slowly, sometimes swiftly when there would arise a leader of superior ability. Of these some had the Power, and then we came out of hiding and wrought as much as we could. Others taught that man must depend upon his hands and the work of those, instead of upon his inner spirit and the controls of that. And then we were not listened to.

"But this we learned not long ago—that time moves not only in one dimension, passing us by like a ribbon drawn too fast for our catching. No, time embraces much more, so that this world in which we move lies close to other worlds existing in the same space, yet separated from us by the walls of this other kind of time. So that there are worlds in which Amun does not exist—as you tell me it does not in your world."

"Space-time continuums!" Tallahassee stared at Jayta. "But that theory is only fiction, used in stories of my time for imaginative entertainment!"

"However you may think of it, we have proved it true. Are you not here in Amun?"

Tallahassee ran her tongue over lips that seemed suddenly dry. Fantastic, insane? . . . What other words could she find to explain such a suggestion? Yet it was plain Jayta was entirely serious.

"Accept that it is so," continued the Priestess, "and know that a year ago one Khasti found a way to breach the wall of that time—for the purpose of ruining Amun itself!"

Her deepset eyes sparked fire, and she seemed even in her mind-to-mind speech to spit forth the name "Khasti" as if it were an obscenity.

"Two treasures have we possessed from the earliest days when we first fled to Kush, we of the most ancient people. This is the truth—an object upon which the Power has been so long focused becomes in turn a reservoir of that force, sometimes to the extent that only those, by training and blood immune to it, can touch it and live."

"The Rod." Tallahassee glanced at the case on the bed. "The Rod into which has entered the centuries of thought-force of those of the Blood. Even I, who can control the Key-to-Life, dare not lay bare hand on that."

"Then why can I?" challenged Tallahassee.

"That I do not know, though I have two guesses, the first being that in your world you are the same as the Princess Ashake, she who gave her life to regain that which had been stolen. The other is that because you *are* from that world, your inner force is of a different nature, repelling rather than attracting the Power that is bound within this. But that is another matter. I must tell you what else you should know and quickly—we may not have time, much time. And there are those who will be alerted once they know that the Rod has returned.

"It was taken by a creature of Khasti because Khasti himself stands behind the late Pharoah's son, Userkof. We have had many queens, and they rule by their own right, not under the will of any man. If they take a husband he is one apart and cannot command in their name. Nor can this Userkof, which is a sore thing to him. For our Candace was the eldest child of King Pahfor's sister and thus the heir.

"The new people among us—those who are restless and would put away the heritage of our past—they strive to follow foreign ways. And Idieze, she who is chief wife to Userkof, would be queen. Thus she plays for power with Khasti and his knowledge.

"The creature of Khasti was sent into the world beyond the time wall and there he was to hide the Rod. There he was freed to draw upon the strength of those of Khasti's own way of thought—those who hated the rule of women —for his energy and aid. Thus the Candace could not come before the people at the Half-Year Feasting with it in her hand. And because of that theft, she could be lied into the loss of her throne. But, Khasti was not as secret as he thought and, when the Rod indeed disappeared, there was a way of learning what he had done and why. However, it took us much searching and experimenting before we could ourselves dare to hope to unlock the same door. And the Key, which we held—that, at a last moment, was itself taken—with dead guards left to mark that we had once held it. For the Key and the Rod are linked, and one can point always the way to the other.

"It was made plain to us that one with power to hold the Rod and to mind-search for it must also breach the door of parallel time—though this was a desperate and perhaps deadly thing. And the Princess Ashake, she whose form you wear, swore that it was her venture alone. For the Candace could not be risked, and there is no other of the whole Blood in this generation, so thin have our ranks now become. Thus we went to the most holy place where the vibrations of the Power had long been, and there she threw herself into the unknown. There she must also have met the full force of some hate like unto Khasti's."

Carey? Tallahassee's thought caught and held upon the man who had made so plain his dislike. . . . It could well be Carey, influenced beyond his knowledge or belief, had been the hostile focus.

"When she returned"—Jayta paused, and then went on—"it would seem that because you, too, had laid hand on the Rod, she must draw you with her. And this was too great a strain on the Talent we had summoned to our backing. Thus she was gone from us, even as she fulfilled the mighty task she had bent herself to do. Also—there was that creature of Khasti's who would have followed her—perhaps it was necessary for her to strive with him also in your time. For he came after—but"—there was complete satisfaction in Jayta's thought now—"him I was able to seal outside now that Key and Rod had returned. I know not if his master has managed to draw him back by whatever unhallowed means he employs, but if he has—then Khasti knows what we have done. Also Userkof knows, for it was the personal guards of his household who broke in upon us at Meroë and were forced to acknowledge that they had no right of intrusion upon the Daughter of the Blood."

At least there was logic in Jayta's explanation, wild as it might seem to Tallahassee. If she could accept this all as reality, then the fact of her sudden transportation here was true.

"What do you want of me?" she asked.

An expression of surprise altered the harsh cast of Jayta's features for a moment.

"Need you ask? The Candace, who knows all of this— save of Ashake's death (though word of that is already on the way to her) is in the north on a state visit to the People of the Sea. She will return in time for the Half-Year Feast. We must then have the Rod ready for her hand. But to all others you must be Ashake! Those who were with us at Meroë are of the second circle of Believers and servers. They are sworn to a still tongue on this business for I needed their united power with mine to light the way for Ashake's return. But in Amun you are the Princess Heir and must be—"

"And if I choose not to aid your plans? I was drawn into this through no will of my own—"

"How?" countered Jayta.

Tallahassee found herself telling of the wild night's work in the museum and how she had been compelled to follow the ankh to the rod, of the presences she had felt during that strange struggle of wills.

"Khasti's creature. It was he who stole the Key and hid it so. It was he who hoped to reach the Rod before the Princess broke through to claim it. It was he who had you lay hand upon it, and so brought her to her death."

"You say his 'creature'. What do you mean?" Tallahassee asked.

For a moment or two she believed that Jayta was not going to answer. Then the message came with obvious reluctance.

"We do not know by what means Khasti has learned of this thing, or how he projected his servant with the Rod into this other world of yours and in turn sent the Key after it. He has set up shields about his work of a kind we cannot pierce. And those who are of our Talent dare not try to spy on him, for they can be instantly detected by some trick of his own kind of power, as we discovered when the Rod vanished. To be unmasked by Khasti is death—we think—for none we sent returned, and neither could we after pick them up by personna-scanner. They —they simply vanished. But his servant who did this thing—he, she, or it—could not have been of the Talent. For that, too, would have registered on those devices our mind-watchers maintain. We do know only that there must have been some alteration in the messenger-thief he sent. You say that the Princess you saw only as a shadow, and this other was also a shadow—a wraith in your world. Well"—again there was satisfaction in Jayta's voice—"that other remains a wraith, since the Key has been turned against the creature's return!"

"If I play this part you wish"—Tallahassee stared straight into the woman's eyes as she formulated that thought with all the force she could summon—"then when it is done and your Queen safe once more, can you return me to my own time?"

"I give you the truth. As it stands now, I am uncertain. But if Userkof is vanquished and all is safe—it may be that the Candace herself can do this thing. If so—she will have the backing in power of all of us who command the Talent."

"But you are not sure?" persisted the girl.

"I am not sure," agreed the priestess. "What we can

do, that we shall. There is this—we must do something, or all we have accomplished so far will be lost."

There was a strong determination in that, and Tallahassee felt a new wariness.

"What?"

"You must become Ashake—not only outwardly, as you are now but inwardly—owning her memories and knowledge."

Tallahassee could see the sense of that, but it would take some time, and how good would she be at learning the language, all the small details of the life of the girl she had replaced? Did they have weeks?

"It will take some time—"

Jayta shook her head. "We cannot give you the Talent if you are not born with it. But all else can be shifted mind-to-mind from our archives—"

"The what?"

"The storehouse of knowledge possessed by all those who follow the way of Power, also those of the Blood who come to rule. The Rod." She gestured to the box. *"That* is theirs by right, but it does not enrich their memories. Rather do all of us with the Talent come twice yearly to the shrine, and there cast our memories into the lap of the Great Power. Thus if I must know what the Daughter-of-Apedemek who was before me at an earlier time understood, I go to this storehouse and draw forth the memory of one who may have lived two lifetimes ago and wore the Golden Mask. What the Princess Ashake knew, you must have—"

"Computer memory banks!" Tallahassee interrupted, excited that she could make such an identification with her own time.

"I do not understand," Jayta returned. "The picture in your mind—it is strange—like unto those things which Khasti has turned to. But in another time-world, who knows what form knowledge takes? There is one more whom we must admit to your secret, since only he will have power enough to use my seal and unlock for use Ashake's recordings. I have already summoned him, and if luck favors us he will be here before daybreak. Now I urge you—eat, sleep, rest well, for what lies before you is no little task. We use such recordings only for a few facts. You must absorb many upon many and those as quickly as possible."

Jayta took the button from her own ear, coiled the line, and laid it neatly upon the top of the box sitting between them. At a clap of her hands, Idia entered and bowed.

Tallahassee was at last able to shed the wig, her head feeling curiously light without its stifling weight. But when she glanced at her shorn skull in the mirror, she was a little startled. Did she look really *that* bad without hair? She wished that the ladies of Amun had not held to that particular legacy from Egypt. Another curtained door gave upon a bath wherein she was glad to plunge, washing away the remaining grit of the desert, though she noted that the skin dye they had laid on her in the temple did not disappear in turn. When she had wrapped around her a loose, long square of soft cotton and gone back to the other room, she found Idia setting out a tray of dishes that contained a small roasted bird, some fruit which Tallahassee identified as slices of melon and small, reddish bananas, and bread which came in thin sheets spread with what could only be a conserve of dates.

It was dark now and, with the coming of the darkness, there glowed two candle-shaped sticks of light, on which no flames danced. Instead, radiance was diffused from along their length. Idia left her alone, and Tallahassee had time to think as she ate. If she could accept this first premise of sidewise trips by an unorthodox theory of time travel, then all else *did* fall into place. But now the thoughts of taking on Ashake's carefully preserved memories made her uneasy. It was true that to learn the language would be a vast help. And if she could play the part of princess better by being able to recognize the proper people and places, she would be safer than she was now. But it remained to be seen just how she took this crash course and how it would change her own mind.

Dare she really risk any such meddling? She would demand from Jayta a complete summary of what such an action would entail when she saw the priestess again. Finishing the meal, Tallahassee moved slowly around the room, studying the fittings on the dressing table. Once she put out her hand to open one of the drawers and then refrained. She did not feel, for all her curiosity concerning the girl she was now supposed to be, that she had any right to pry in this way.

There was a soft *"puurtt"* and under the edge of the outer door curtain padded first one and then the other of the kittens she had met in the garden. They seemed at home here, falling into a follow-the-leader game of leaping on the bed, prancing across it, then jumping from its end to the top of the dressing table where they landed with ease, threading in and out, with the air of long practice, among the bottles and jars there. At last they returned to the bed and curled up, one of them eyeing Tallahassee sleepily over the other's rounded back as if asking why she did not join them.

But she felt far from sleepy. The length of cloth she had found lying on a bench beside the bath was hardly attire to go venturing forth in. And she had no wish to assume again the wig which now sat on a stand before the mirror—the lifted cobra head of the diadem seeming to watch her knowingly with small, jeweled eyes. When Idia returned for the supper tray, she smiled at Tallahassee reassuringly and held out one hand to cup the candle lamp, though her flesh did not touch its radiant surface. As she drew her fingers downward along it, the light faded. Tallahassee understood the pantomimed instruction, smiled in return, and nodded.

All at once she did begin to feel sleepy. It had been a long day—or maybe days. For the first time she wondered, as she slipped out of the cloth and into the bed, trying not to disturb the kittens, what had happened back in her own time and place. What excuse would they have for her being missing? Could they think she had taken both their mysterious find and the rod? Dr. Carey, for one, she believed would never credit what had happened. Perhaps it was better for her that she had come through and not been left to face him with the wild story she would have had to tell when the real Ashake did her disappearing act.

One of the kittens shifted position and laid its head on her leg as if that were a pillow. This was real, here and now, she could never deny that any more. And so she drifted into sleep more quickly than she would have believed possible.

Tallahassee awoke with a weight on her chest and opened her eyes a little dazedly to look upward into a kitten face. The small mouth shaped an impatient mew, and she saw that sunlight entered the room in broad shafts from under the door curtain. Only a moment later Makeda came in. It was plain she was disturbed for she began to gesture as soon as she saw that Tallahassee was watching her, making the motions of getting up as if there was some need for hurry.

The kitten hissed as the girl put it gently to one side to slip out of bed. Makeda gestured again—this time to the door of the bath. Again Tallahassee found water drawn, this time with petals of flowers strewn upon its surface, and two open pots standing nearby, each giving off a strange, sweet scent. She bathed and dried herself on the towel Makeda produced and then, at the other's direction, scooped up fingers of the creamy, scented

lotion from the pot she liked best and rubbed it into her
darkened skin. The odor once applied was not so strong,
but fragrant enough to please.

This time the robe Makeda held ready for her was
not the austere white slip of a priestess, but rather resembled in style the caftan popular in her own world.
The color was clear rose pink, the borders of the wide
sleeves worked about six inches deep with gold thread, a
girdle of gold links settling about her slim hips to mold
the folds closer to her body.

Makeda set to work deftly, applying the heavy eye
make-up. But Tallahassee was glad to see that she did
not reach again for the thick, smothering wig. Instead
the other produced from one of the drawers of the dressing table a small, turban-like cap of gold net and with it
a box from which she took a wide collar that extended
nearly to shoulder point on either side and well down
Tallahassee's breast. This was fashioned of rows of small
flowers, rose quartz, clear crystal, and enameled metal,
the whole set in gold.

Tallahassee studied the result of their combined labors
for the perfect toilet of a princess as Makeda stood back,
having clasped the necklace-collar. Barbaric? Not quite,
she decided. More like a sophisticated playing at bar-
barianism, something akin to those fads that swept the
time she knew, drawing on African, South American,
Mayan designs, in part, for their source. The necklace
was a heavy weight, and she shifted her shoulders, trying to adjust to its presence.

"Ashake!"

A man's voice just outside the door curtain. Makeda's
hand had flown to her lips, her expression was one of
consternation.

"Ashake!" There was a rising impatience in that hail,
and Tallahassee decided that who ever stood there was
not in the mood to be put off. Who would have the famil-

iarity to hail a Princess of the Blood in such a fashion? The cousin who had his eye on the throne? Drawing a quick breath, Tallahassee arose. There was no use in lingering here—sooner or later she was going to have to face whoever impatiently demanded her presence.

She moved to the door. Makeda made a small gesture of defeat. Yet the girl, looking closely at the under-priestess as she passed, thought she did not detect any fear. Or would she be afraid if it was Userkof? Apparently she now agreed with Tallahassee that the stranger must be faced, for she went to sweep aside the door curtain.

Tallahassee, seeing who stood there, froze, but was startled into voicing a name:

"Jason!"

BUT even as Tallahassee spoke that name she knew that this was not the Jason she had known all her life. He wore Jason's features right enough, but he could not be Jason.

"Ashake?" Now he made of her name not a request for her instant company, but rather a question as he stared at her, his expression of pleasure fading into one of puzzlement.

It was hard to believe that the man was not Jason, though the garments he wore, which resembled those of the soldiers who had first invaded the temple (yet were of a different color, a rust-brown, and had embellishments of brilliant gold on the collar and a lion's head on the chest), were certainly nothing pertaining to her Jason. Nor were the wide bands of gold about his wrists, the belt with a precious-metal-hilted dagger riding on one hip.

"Herihor!"

Jayta came skimming down the arched passage that flanked the pool. Like Tallahassee, her head was now covered with a small turban, but she still wore the plain white shift of her office.

He turned his head, and then sketched a salute, as if to the office the older woman held, before bursting into speech which Jayta's upheld hand hastily silenced, as she glanced around as if to make sure that no other listener save Makeda was nearby.

Then she beckoned imperatively, and both Jason (no, Herihor) and Tallahassee followed. They went along beside the pool into another room that held a table piled with sheets of thick paper, some of which were in rolls. While around the walls. . . . Tallahassee under other circumstances would have been eager to explore. Outside of a museum she had never seen such an array of artifacts as lay or stood on shelves that covered the walls from near floor level to ceiling. Jayta indicated a chair to Tallahassee and pushed two stools forward.

The priestess's speech was quick, staccato, and Tallahassee could guess by the slight changes in the man's expression what she must be doing, retelling the events of the immediate past.

At first the girl thought that he refused to accept what he heard. Then he stared at Tallahassee so measuringly that she was certain he did now believe the priestess's account. Perhaps in this world such things were not uncommon. And as his expression changed, he became less and less like Jason. There was a grimness in the set of his mouth that she had never seen her cousin wear. Twice his hand snapped, as if instinctively, to the hilt of the dagger at his belt, as if he could hardly control the urge to draw that weapon. To use against *her?* There had been a note in his voice, when first he hailed her, that suggested some emotional tie with the Ashake who had been.

Now he listened so intently to what Jayta said that her

words might have been a verdict affecting him deeply. When the priestess had done he answered in an even, cold voice, never glancing at Tallahassee. Then he arose and stalked from the room, again bringing her a fleeting memory of Jason who also had just such an expressive way of holding his shoulders when he was annoyed, whether he might give voice to that annoyance or not.

Jayta watched him go, half raising her hand as if to stop him. Then she shook her head, seemingly at her own thoughts, and once more beckoned to Tallahassee.

Back they went to the girl's own room where Makeda and Idia had moved two of the small tables together beside the bed, in order to support a box from which led covered wire cords. This was not the same equipment that they had used for communication, for both cords this time were attached to a single circlet. Jayta motioned Tallahassee to the bed and reached out herself to take off the small turban before the girl was well aware of what she would do.

Tallahassee eyed the circlet warily. She did not care for the idea of using it as apparently the priestess meant it to be used. But did she honestly have any choice? She could not go on blindly here. And if this arrangement would fill in facts for her, give her the knowledge she lacked, then she did not really dare to refuse it. Only she wanted to get away even as Jayta adjusted the band about her forehead and pushed her down on the narrow bed.

From Makeda, the priestess took a very small bottle and thrust a pin into one end sealed with a covering of taut skin. With one swift gesture, before Tallahassee could elude her, she swung the bottle under the girl's nose. Queer aromatic smell . . .

Tallahassee brought no one clear memory out of that induced sleep when she opened her eyes to see Idia seated on a stool near the head of the bed. The—there had been something on her head, hadn't there? But it was gone now. . . .

The memory inducer!

"The dream is over, Great Lady."

"It is." Then Tallahassee realized that she had answered in the same tongue as the question had been asked.

She was—she was Ashake of the Blood. But she was someone else, too. She frowned as she tried to fit one memory to another. Idia had hurried away, beyond the curtain. That machine, it was gone.

This was—she sat up on the bed, discovering an odd weakness in her body, as if she had been ill and was just trying out her legs, having been bed-bound for some time. This was her room. She could look upon each item in it as old and long familiar, some cherished because of past associations. But those were of Ashake's memories not hers, another part of her mind made haste to report. At least one fear she had held had not been realized—she, herself, had not lost her own identity, no matter how clearly she could now call upon a dead woman's past recollections.

Only . . . her head ached and she held it. So much . . . she needed time—time to sort out what lay there. And there had come fear with those memories, no longer for herself, but that fear which had been the Princess's, the fear that had, at last, driven Ashake to take the dangerous venture which ended in her death.

"It is done?" It was not a statement but a question. Jayta entered the chamber with her swift, gliding step.

"I remember—too much . . ." Tallahassee replied.

"There cannot be too much, Great Lady. For you have a part to play, not only before those who love you and wish you well, but also those who watch for that which can be used against you. We have less time than we thought. Also, there has been a spy beam set upon us, cutting us off from contact with the temple at New Napata. While the news the Prince General brought . . ."

She paced up and down as might the lioness, which she had seemed in part to be at their first meeting, might do when pent within a cage. There was more than impatience in her expression. There rested there now an urgency approaching distress.

"You must listen to the Prince." She turned abruptly once more to Tallahassee. "His spies have brought him news that is worse than ever we dreamed."

Herihor, Ashake's memory identified the Prince. Not Jason—Herihor. He was of the Blood, but lesser, a leader of men who was general of the border forces to the north. And—he had been betrothed to Ashake from the time they were very young, though they could not wed until those of the Greater Learning allowed the Princess to retire from that service.

"I—I cannot think clearly," Tallahassee protested, rubbing the forehead of her aching head with the palms of both hands as if she could so banish the pain.

"Makeda brings a healing draught. Drink it all, Great Lady. I wish you might indeed rest away this day. But time passes—we cannot now know what happens elsewhere while we are here. The Candace—there is a message that out-of-season storms in the desert lands prevent her flight back. She may be so late that the Half-Year Feast will be upon us before she arrives. The Prince General has sent two of his most trusted officers with messages for her. Neither has reported back. We are told all communications are affected by these storms. But those who handle the sending may well already be creatures of Userkof. May the jaws of Set open wide for him!"

The under-priestess returned carrying a goblet and knelt to hand it to Tallahassee. She sniffed doubtfully at the odor of the colorless liquid, but memory sustained her guess that this was only a restorative.

And Jason—Herihor—came even as she drank deeply, making a face at the bitter taste. His expression was set, and he did not meet her eyes, gazing over and beyond her. If he really cared for Ashake, and memory now insisted that he had, he must resent her. Tallahassee felt a faint regret about that as he swept so swiftly into speech, she believed he wanted to say what must be said and then get quickly away from sight of her.

"I cannot break the spy beam," he began tersely. "But there is no mistake, it comes from the southwest. And the Fourth Ashanti force lies between us and Napata."

Out of her memory sprang a name. "Itua?" Tallahassee asked.

Herihor nodded. "Itua and perhaps Ukaya also. I know not how far the rot has extended. There was a certainty that Khasti had a meeting—secretly—with both our esteemed relatives and a picked handful of the army. It was noted that they did not summon General Shabaoko or Marshal Nastasen. Nor did Colonel Namlia know until too late to station any of her guards. They dared to enter the South Palace without proper authority. And"—he shrugged—"they had something that repelled any of our devices. Khasti has promised much in the way of new equipment, and he may now be producing it. Two of my best men sent to keep an eye on them have vanished—even their personna check does not suggest where they are—"

"Dead?" Tallahassee fought to call upon the proper memories to understand what he was saying.

"No—at least the personna has not erased them. And I have had the best looker in search on this plane."

A looker, Ashake's memory supplied, was one trained in the strange and, to Tallahassee, non-understandable lore of the temples, wherein apparently psychometry, hardly yet understood in *her* world, could be put to definite and concrete use to locate people.

"I went to Zyhlarz." Now Herihor was pacing back and forth in the same caged fashion the priestess had earlier shown. "He says that what Khasti is using does not fit any device born from the Great Knowledge, and that even with the accented Power, *he,* himself, cannot catch the minds, now, of more than half of the suspected officers and councillors."

There was an exclamation from Jayta. "What has this one of Set done that he can stand against the Greater Knowledge?"

"That is within your province, not mine, Daughter-of-Apedemek," Herihor snapped. "I only know that three flyers striving to hover over the South Palace crashed. And their pilots were dead when we found them. I have done everything, save call out what troops I am sure of. Those are mainly the Candace's own guard and the north forces. We may have to try such action officially before the end of this—to batter down the gate by force of arms, though to do so might well bring down upon us the very revolt we fear. Naldamak *must* return. I have alerted the Guard. But what Khasti has . . ." He flung out his hands. "He might even be able to bring down the flyer carrying her, though we have been testing with that thought in view these past two days. It would seem that whatever influence he has under his control, its range of force is yet limited. We were fools not to keep a better guard on him from the start. Fools!" He drove one fist into the palm of his other hand.

"That is what comes"—he rounded on Jayta as if he was accusing her of some crime—"of believing too much in one way of Power. Khasti has gone beyond the Great Knowledge, I will swear to that!"

"He depends upon the work of men's hands." Jayta looked as angry as the Prince. "Man cannot stand alone without the aid of that which is beyond."

"No? Tell that to my dead men, Daughter-of-

Apedemek. They are dead, thrown out of the air as if they were leaves whirled off in a storm. And it was *not* a power of the Greater Knowledge that did that! Nor can Zyhlarz, who is supposed to draw to him the height of your knowledge, explain it even to himself. Khasti must be stopped—but tell me how? I will not send more men uselessly into a death trap."

Jayta appeared to have controlled her momentary flash of temper. "We have done what we came to do. The Rod and the Key are safe in our hands—"

"At the cost of another death!" he flung at her.

"If it would cost us all the Circle of the Talent, still we must have so spent their lives," she replied calmly.

"I know," he said in a low voice. "I know why she had to go. But that makes her loss no easier to bear. And what if the Key and the Rod are *not* the answer? What if whatever Khasti has discovered is greater—"

"No!" Jayta's voice rang out fiercely. "A hundred centuries of years have we wrought within ourselves to achieve what we know. I will not believe that there is some thing of metal that can counter the Greater Knowledge, wherein we work with that which powers this world itself! If this man tries such—"

"I am not of the Temple, Daughter-of-Apedemek," Herihor answered curtly. "And I have seen in the past what the Belief of the Chosen Ones can accomplish. Have they not made the desert bloom and bear fruit, strengthened our race until we stand staunch against the barbarians, north and south? No man denies that this has been done, is being done. But if Khasti has made himself master of something else, then we must accept that perhaps even the Greater Knowledge can be threatened."

The Greater Knowledge. Tentatively Tallahassee, listening only a little to the dispute before her, tried to tap memory (or series of memories) concerning the nature of that. But while the life of Amun and her place in it came

clearly to the surface when she called it, this other. . . .
No, to summon it was like trying to catch wisps of flying
shadows between her hands. Perhaps the Princess did
not record that, it might be considered too secret to have
where such might be drawn upon.

She could pick out the history of this time level from
her memory induction. Egypt, which in her own world
had been rumored by so many cults to be the fountainhead
of occult knowledge, had, on this plane, indeed discovered and perfected a type of mental control and general ESP (centered in a trained priesthood and the royal
family) which did approach that ability the cults argued it
once had had.

Though Egypt had fallen to invaders, first Greek and
then Roman, even as in her own world's history, it had
not been lost. Retreating south to Kush, the modern
Sudan, those of the Hierarchy who had survived again
brought their civilization to a peak, favoring their own
teaching. Arabs had attempted to invade from modern
Ethiopia but they had been driven off during a war that
had again depleted the hard core of the priesthood—for
the strained use of their powers had brought death or
mental collapse to many. So Meroë had fallen, while the
handful of refugees—the royal family and what was left
of those with the Knowledge—had fled westward.

There were very few in any following generation who
showed ability for the training that the closed Circle of
the Talented kept alive. Thus their ranks of late were
thin, though a generation after their westward flight, a
king of unusual ability had come to the throne. After the
custom of those of the Blood from the most ancient of
days, he married his half sister, one who had passed three
of the four stages toward becoming a major wielder of
the Power. Together they had laid the foundations for the
Empire. It seemed an auspicious time, now looked back
upon as a golden age, for there had been then, for a short

interval, a number of births of those having the Talent, and several of these were also rulers of provinces that the outspreading Empire occupied.

There followed a peak of prosperity and success that lasted for nearly two centuries. But what favored their safety was the fact that in this world there had arisen no Mohammed, no way of Islam to drown in blood the central African states, as had happened in the history Tallahassee knew.

Coptic Christianity spread slowly among the lower classes, but the hard inner core of the rulers and administrators remained almost fanatically tied to the Great Knowledge. And in the royal family a strain of those who had the Talent continued.

Europe, Tallahassee had learned from her new foster memory, had not meddled. Though trading ships from Portugal, Spain, and England visited Empire ports, the northerners had not dared to attempt that conquest which had brought the curse of the slave trade to this continent. For by the time Europeans made their appearances, the Empire was close-locked with India, China, and the Far East in bonds of trade. Since there was no interruption of the Meroë-Egyptian civilization, their own inventions and defenses equalled if not topped those of the traders.

Cunning metal workers always, and led by the Great Knowledge that planned and experimented, those of Amun had developed a modern civilization on a par with any of the emerging African nations of her world, yet far more stable because of the core of belief on which they had drawn for centuries. Now at last, they were being threatened, not from without, but from within. Again, there had been a marked recession of Talented births. Ashake had been the only one of the royal line to possess the Power for two generations. And, because such were weak in numbers, there came suggestions that the rulers of Amun apply other means for their defense.

Tradition here was a power in itself, so, at first, Khasti found few to listen to him. It was the envy of Userkof and the real hatred of his chief wife for his royal cousins, whose attainments were higher than she dared to hope to equal—that gave Khasti his chance. His own background was obscure, for he had only appeared several years ago, shunning the temple but prevailing on Userkof for support.

Jayta drew herself up proudly. "No work of any mind not endowed with the grace of that Which is Beyond Measurement can stand. Where it is used, there will it break the tie between us and the earth. Look at those to the north with their constant warring, their famines, their plagues. . . . Have the people of Amun faced such in a hundred hundred years? We open our hearts to all life about us, and through us, then, the spirit of life flows into the hands of the farmer who tends the grain, the herdsman with his flocks. Our people dream beauty, and it comes alive under their fingers. Do we plant a tree and leave it to live or die—no. He who plants draws into him the spirit of life which he wills outward again to aid the growing roots under the soil. We are builders and not destroyers—and if we turn from the truth we shall indeed be lost."

"How many have now the Great Knowledge?" Herihor flung the question at her. "How many children are born in these days who can be brought to temple care and nurtured to the use of the Talent? What if we grow too old, our blood too thin? What if there comes a time when this life-spirit cannot be summoned?"

"There are ebbs and flows of the tide," Jayta returned. "If we stand now at an ebb, there will come a flow. But it is now that those who believe against us will strike. For it is as you say, our numbers are not great. Therefore, we must attack first, root out this Khasti and the abominations with which he busies himself."

"If we can," Herihor commented darkly.

"Look upon what we have already done," Jayta said sharply. "Were we sure we could find where the Rod was hidden? Yet that we did, even though the Key was also stolen. It is back in our hold. And I tell you, my Prince, that the Rod is far more than many believe it to be."

"Just what do you mean by that? It is a symbol of authority, and it seems true that no one not of the true line of the Blood can hold it. But what else is it?" he demanded.

"We do not know yet," she told him frankly. "But there was a power unleashed in it even as we drew it back that we do not yet understand. Or perhaps"—she looked to Tallahassee sitting silent on the bed—"that was the doing of someone else."

"I have nothing of your Talent," the girl quickly denied. "You have given me enough of *her* memory so I know what I lack."

Herihor glanced from her to Jayta and back again, his eyes now searching Tallahassee's painted face as if beneath that cosmetic mask he could find a truth he must have.

"Yes, Daughter-of-Apedemek—your number of supporters lacks now the one I think you esteemed the highest of all. By so much are you the loser." There was bitterness in his voice, and his eyes were cold, his expression closed. Did he really hate her? Tallahassee was sure that that must be the truth.

"We do not know what we face." Jayta seemed to temporize. "It is only true that above all else we must hold in safety the Rod and the Key and pray that the Candace finds a quick way home. Since the spy ray holds us mute, perhaps it is better to send some messenger directly to the Temple to speak with Zyhlarz. And guards—"

"I know my trade. I brought the Ibex Regiment with me when I came. And two messages have gone to those commanders I can still trust in full. One answered while I was still airborne. He is moving overland to keep open the north road—if he can. For if Khasti extends this power of his, who knows what evil surprises we shall have to face."

He gave a quick nod of his head, divided between the two of them, and was gone before the priestess could speak again. Tallahassee broke the silence between them with a question she was herself surprised to hear, even as she asked it:

"Did he love her very much?"

For a second or two Jayta appeared so buried in some thought of her own that it did not register. Then she started, stared at Tallahassee, so that the girl had a queer, shamed feeling, as if the question she had asked broke some important rule of politeness.

"The Prince Herihor was chosen as consort for the Princess," Jayta's tone was very remote and forbidding, "since he was not of the pure Blood. It was believed that perhaps a mixture of such heritage would strengthen anew the line for the next generation. It is—was—Ashake's child who would wear the next crown."

A marriage of convenience and state, then. Yet Tallahassee thought that that greeting shouted outside her bedroom earlier had held something else, a warmth of feeling. But she could not judge these people, she told herself firmly. She might have Ashake's memories filtered through their recall machine, but she did not possess any concerning Herihor that seemed especially close. In fact, she was now engrossed by a discovery she had just made—there were no overtones of emotion raised by any of those memories she had yet sampled. She was not aware that Jayta, having watched her closely for a breath or two, went silently out of the room. For

Tallahassee was testing, after a fashion, those memories, drawing to the fore of her mind each of the people she was supposed to be closely allied with, to wait some response, a yes or no of liking—no matter how faint. And still she could detect none at all.

$\mathcal{T}$ALLAHASSEE'S headache dulled, she was able to eat all of the meal Idia brought her later and knew her energy was flowing back. In fact she felt almost euphoric, a condition that aroused suspicion in her mind. Had the restorative also been a drug of sorts to tie her more closely to Jayta's will? She could not detect a ground for such suspicion in the Ashake memories she could tap. But it was well not to depend too much on those for present assurance.

She went out beside the pool and sat on a bench, gazing into the water where the lotus blossoms spread wide their pointed petals. This was her own villa, or Ashake's, she knew now, a private retreat where the Princess had many times withdrawn for study and meditation in the past. Within it she was as secure—as long as she *was* Ashake—as she could be anywhere in this world.

The kittens came leaping out of nowhere to jump up

beside her. One spoke in feline fashion at some length, staring straight up into Tallahassee's face as if delivering some message. When she put out her hand, it nipped delicately at her fingertips, while the other small mouth yawned wide, as, sleepy-eyed, it settled down for a nap.

This was soothing. She could almost push away that feeling of displacement. Would Ashake grow stronger in her and become dominant? Tallahassee stirred uneasily. How much dared she give open passage in her mind to those implanted memories?

There was—

Tallahassee stiffened, tense. Both cats roused, turned on the bench to stare at some point behind her. Both wrinkled their lips in silent snarls. The girl's hand went to the hilt of the dagger at her waist. Behind her—now—was danger.

She made herself rise slowly as if unaware. A call would bring one of the Amazon guard. Only there was something . . . This she had felt before, not as a Princess of Amun but rather as herself, Tallahassee Mitford.

Slowly she turned to face what lurked there. Though this was day and not in a dark building in another time and world, there was again that presence—no better could she describe it. Only she could see nothing. . . .

Nothing? No! In the doorway of that chamber where Jayta had her roles of wisdom—there flickered a shadow. And that shadow . . .

Tallahassee could not define it as more than a kind of blurring of her own sight, a blurring confined to that one area. Drawing upon every bit of courage she possessed, the girl started toward it. Her hand moved, not by her will, but directed by the Ashake memory, in a gesture, to draw in the air the outline of the Key.

There was—not menace, she realized, as her own controlled fear began to ebb. Here was a need that reached her fleetingly. And then that blur was gone. As if a door had closed. What kind of a door and why? Ashake was dead. It could not have been the Princess's shadow-self that invaded Tallahassee's world and lingered here now. Both memories assured her that was impossible.

But there had been that other one. The curdling in the air among the ruins when Jayta had sent such a presence away. The other one—he or she who had been dispatched by this Khasti to steal and hide the greatest defense of Amun—could such be the lurker? If so—they might face a danger now that even all the vaunted Ancient Knowledge could not handle. For when an enemy is invisible . . .

Tallahassee made herself go to that doorway, gaze into the room beyond. But she knew the thing had gone. The cold chill of fear that it could bring with it was already fading. However, that it went did not mean it would not return.

"Great Lady?"

Tallahassee was so startled by a voice from behind that she nearly cried out. But she mastered her loss of self-control before she turned to face Colonel Namila, herself.

"Warrior-of-the-lion." The old, old acknowledgment came unbidden from the second memory.

"There is one who has come—the Princess Idieze. She would have speech with the Great Lady."

Idieze—the wife of Userkof—she whose jealousy had brought on much of this trouble here. But why did she come?

"You may admit her to the presence, but summon also the Daughter-of-Apedemek and Prince General Herihor."

"As it is commanded, so it is done." The Amazon gave the formal response.

Tallahassee moved back to the bench, deliberately seated herself. She guessed that Idieze might come so boldly on a kind of "fishing" expedition. She had both the cunning and the arrogance to take such action. Ashake's memory supplied much concerning Idieze and little or none of it good.

There was a stir at the main door at the far end of the pool as a slender woman wearing a garment of saffron yellow and a small travel wig came determinedly forward, those escorting her lingering by the gate. Tallahassee did not rise to greet her. Ashake's rank was far higher than that of this upstart female. In the old days, before the smothering etiquette of the court had been revised, this one would have approached on hands and knees and kissed the sandal strip of the Princess. None of the Blood ran in her veins.

If no emotion had broken through from the memories Tallahassee had earlier sifted, she had been wrong in feeling that none such existed. For the very sight of Idieze's smooth, painted face brought to life now a flare of hot anger.

The woman was very beautiful, her lips finely chiseled, her features well cut. Though she was small and dainty, yet she had excellent carriage and she held herself with that inborn assurance which beauty breeds in a woman. Even as contemptuous as Ashake's memories were, Tallahassee knew that the Princess had always understood the appeal Idieze had for her weakling cousin, and how this perfection in flesh could mold him easily to her purpose.

"I see you, Idieze." Tallahassee-Ashake gave greeting, not of intimate to intimate, equal to equal, but rather of the Blood to the lesser. And she saw the swiftly hidden spark in Idieze's eyes. It was as if something in Tallahassee now fed triumphantly on the hate the other projected.

"The Great Lady receives her servant." The other's voice was soft, carrying no hint of anger. Idieze was a superb actress, Tallahassee had to admit.

There was the sound of sandals and boots on the pavement behind. The girl did not need to look around to know that Namlia had carried out orders. Jayta and Herihor were coming. She wanted no confrontation with this—this viper that was not witnessed by those she could trust.

"Greeting, Daughter-of-Apedemek," Idieze continued. "And to you, General of the North." She smiled gently. "Has some emergency arisen that you are called from your station when the Glorious-in-the-Sun Naldamak is not with us?"

"I did not realize, Lady, that your interest in military matters was so marked." Herihor's voice was cool.

She only smiled, warmly and graciously. "Is not my Lord, also, of the defenses of our land?" she countered sweetly. "As his wife, I have learned much."

That you have, Tallahassee thought, or perhaps should it not more rightly be that he has learned from *you!*

Impatience stirred in her. Idieze would not come here without a purpose. Let them get to the point quickly. Though she could trust her implanted memory, yet there was something about this female that was a threat she could well do without and speedily. It might not follow the rules of formality and custom, but she decided now to dispense with those.

"You have sought me out, Idieze," Tallahassee said bluntly, "and for that there must be a reason."

"Concern for your welfare, Great Lady. It has been rumored in New Napata that you have been grievously ill—"

"So?" Tallahassee was aware of that searching glance the other gave her. She wondered what *had* really been told Idieze, what had been the result on the enemies' side of that invasion into the other world? Had they even suspected the real result—Ashake's death? If so, Idieze must be confounded now, through she showed no trace of surprise.

"Rumor," she continued deliberately, "often is fathered and mothered by false reports. As you see, my health is good. As one of the Talented I withdraw to renew my spirit—as all know must be done at intervals."

"When the Graciousness-in-the-Sun and her sister of the Blood are both gone, and none is delegated to hold the Rod, there is uneasiness." Idieze still smiled with her mouth, kept her voice low and gentle, but Tallahassee wished she could see more clearly into those downcast eyes.

"And to whom would the Rod pass," Tallahassee asked in a voice she hoped was as deceptively mild as the other's, "seeing that there are none of the pure Blood to set hand to it?"

The smile was gone now, the lips set straightly together, as if the other had an answer that prudence alone kept her from saying aloud.

"But"—Tallahassee was being forced to this because Ashake's memory warned her that she dared not trepass too deeply on a field of action adverse to the ways of the court—"since you have come in your concern, you are greeted. The way to New Napata is long, and it is close to evening. You are bidden to dine, to sleep within these walls, you and your people."

It did not sound very gracious, and she did not mean it to. Also she heard a slight stir from the direction of Herihor, behind her left shoulder, and she knew that perhaps he was not pleased with what she had done. But to send Idieze forth now would mean an open break that perhaps they could not afford. Tallahassee clapped her hands, and as two maid servants appeared she gave orders.

"Escort the Lady Idieze to the guest quarters. See also that those who serve her are made at ease."

Idieze smiled again, and at the sight of that a small doubt arose in Tallahassee. The woman wanted to stay, she had come here for no other reason. Why? Now she made a graceful gesture of homage and withdrew, walking down the other side of the pool toward rooms at the back of the villa, her people coming from the gateway to follow her. Two maids and another woman, older and somewhat hunched of back, who hobbled along leaning on a cane. Yes, that was the old crone Idieze had ever about her. Some said she was the ancient nurse who had tended her as a child—others retailed more fantastic suggestions.

"She comes for a purpose." Herihor spoke first, staring after that ordered withdrawal as Tallahassee arose and turned to face the other two.

"Better," Jayta remembered, "that she be under our own eyes now. Our Lady could not turn her from the door, even though there lies no friendship between them. It may be that we can learn what has brought her here."

"Learn anything from that one?" Herihor laughed harshly. "She is like the scorpion hiding beneath a rock, her sting raised—yet the shadow of the rock ever hides her threat. I do not like it."

"Neither do I," returned Tallahassee as frankly. "But, as Jayta says, what else could be done with her? We do not yet court an open break with her party. Let the Daughter-of-Apedemek deal with the matter; there is perhaps something that can be done by the Talent to learn more."

Jayta nodded. "Yes. For now, we must be content with the matter as it stands. It would be well to acquaint Colonel Namlia with a suggestion that the guard of honor be doubled tonight—"

"With special emphasis on the outer part of the guest quarters." When Herihor's left brow slid up as Jason's had so often, for a moment Tallahassee's heart lifted. If

he only *were* Jason! If she could have confidence that he
did not hold any grudge against her, that he was not just
serving her because it was his duty!

"We must all do our best," were the only words that
came to her lips. She was not looking forward to this disturbing night wherein she must fence with Idieze across
food she had now little desire to taste.

At least they did not share the same table, and there
was nearly the width of the room between them. For it
seemed that the household at the villa followed the old
Egyptian custom of food being served on small, separate
tables, each placed beside a chair. Tallahassee, Herihor,
Jayta, and Idieze were grouped at one end of the room,
while members of the household of sufficient rank were a
little apart. Among the latter there was easy if low-voiced
conversation, though it did not include the hunched form
near the opposite door—Idieze's crone attendant. But
among those of rank there was a general silence as if
each were only too-well occupied with his or her own
thoughts.

Once or twice Tallahassee had that shivering sensation of being overlooked. She saw Jayta stir, glance over
her shoulder at the painted expanse of the wall at their
backs. Did the priestess also pick up that feeling that
there was something hovering about them? The girl
longed for the meal to be done, for Idieze to be gone, so
she could share with the Daughter-of-Apedemek her curious experience beside the pool.

Only Idieze showed no sign of wanting yet to withdraw. She had finished her meal. Now one of the maids
standing along the wall ready to give service brought
forward a carved box from which the Princess selected a
slender brown stick, putting it to her lips, waiting for the
maid to touch a flame to its tip. Smoke rose in needle-
thin curls from the stick when Idieze drew deeply upon
it, so that a tiny spot of flame flared.

"It is sad that you who followed the Upper Path, Great Lady," she said, "are forbidden so many of the luxuries of life. These pleasant dream sticks can be most soothing to the nerves."

A tendril of the smoke floated in Tallahassee's direction. It was sickly-sweet and, without thinking, she fanned it away.

"Lady," it was Jayta who spoke, "this is a house for those who do follow the Upper Path. Such—"

"Cannot be defiled by my dream stick?" Idieze laughed. "I am rebuked." She thrust the glowing tip into the dregs of wine in her goblet. "Forgive me, Daughter-of-Apedemek. We of the outer world are not so constrained in our life. The old ways"—she gave a dainty shrug—"they fasten chains upon one, and it is so unnecessary. For much can be learned by an open will and mind."

She was insolent, being deliberately so, Tallahassee realized. And why did Idieze feel so free to speak thus—here?

Herihor set down his goblet, his eyes were on Idieze with that narrowed intentness that had been—was—Jason's when he was considering some problem. Tallahassee could believe that he was now as alert as she was to the danger of Idieze and her real purpose in coming here.

It was as if Idieze herself could read that thought. Her lazy smile was gone. Now she leaned forward a little in her chair.

"Great Lady, there is a matter that must be discussed. But, privately . . ." And her eyes shifted to those in the other part of the room.

"So we had guessed," Tallahassee returned. "Let us to the poolside, then."

Herihor was almost instantly at her side, holding out his arm so she could touch fingers to his wrist. As she arose, Tallahassee bowed her head to Jayta, but gave no such courtesy to Idieze. The sooner that one spat out whatever poison she had brought hither, the better. For Ashake, memory was only too clear in reminding what Idieze could do.

Colonel Namlia was by the door as Tallahassee and Herihor reached it. And Tallahassee gave her order.

"We speak in private—by the pool. See that we are undisturbed."

"On my head be it, Great Lady." The Colonel raised her hand to touch the lion emblem to the fore of her linen sphinx headdress.

Two of her Amazons were waved to draw another bench near to the one where Tallahassee had rested earlier. Then they took their places well out of earshot, their backs to the four who sat there, Tallahassee between Herihor and Jayta, Idieze on the smaller bench facing the three bound in what she must see was open hostility against her.

"You would speak, I see you," Tallahassee said.

"Princess, Priestess, General"—Idieze looked slowly from one face to another—"and all so ready to beware one unarmed woman—me. You grant me stature I do not have, Great Lady."

"Be glad then that you do not, for the wrath of the Blood is not a light thing to face." Out of Ashake memory came the words. Yet Idieze was smiling once more, and now she laughed, low and sweetly.

"Such ponderous language, Great Lady. One would think that the Blood was about to pronounce one of those Seven Curses which, we are told, could wither flesh, break bones. It does not matter that I am hated here, but truly I have come out of concern. The Blood has held power a very long time—by ways so ancient that the very accounts are now dreary dust. To everything there comes an end, have you ever thought of that,

Great Lady? Those of the Blood, of the Upper Way are very few now, a handful against perhaps more than half a nation.

"There is no cure for narrowness of mind; that leads only to stagnation and defeat. The end of your road is very near, Great Lady, and if one does not heed the branching of another path ahead, there can follow chaos. None of us wants to see Amun rent by a war of brother against brother, sister against sister. But the branch of the tree which gives not to pull of the storm wind breaks and is gone."

"A warning, Lady?" Tallahassee cut into this spate of metaphors. "So you think you are strong enough to give a warning? That in itself is interesting indeed."

Idieze's smile set a fraction. "You here have had no news from New Napata, I believe, for some hours. There can be many changes in even a small portion of such a space of time, Great Lady."

"And what momentous happening has there been at New Napata in those hours?"

"Changes, Great Lady. Not all love the past. It is said that the Temple of Light is now closed so that none go in or come out again. Rumor can whip the people to violence. And rumor spreads that the Son-of-Apedemek, Zyhlarz himself, has been struck mad so that he howls like a desert jackal and looses upon those of his own people death from the mind. Do not discount rumor, Great Lady, it often holds a core of truth. And do not discount what I have to offer. The turn in the road will not be open for long."

"That turn being a way for Userkof?" Tallahassee asked. "From such a change there could come only trouble. He is not of the direct descent and his get— though I believe you have not yet provided our lord with any to call him father—cannot sit in the Lion's seat."

"So there is no heir save you, Royal Daughter? Ah,

but you are also barred from the throne now since you profess the celibacy of those who strive to follow the Upper Way. And this valiant lord has waited so long for you that already he looks elsewhere!"

She swung on Herihor, there was a sharpness in her features that carried the threat of an aimed dagger. Tallahassee did not doubt that Idieze was about to spew forth something she thought to be true.

"In the old days, General Prince Herihor, our men took more than one wife. Does this Great Lady betrothed to you know the rumors of a white skin from the north who now confidently expects to wear jewels of your bestowing?"

Herihor made a slight movement but his face was smooth of any telltale expression. "Your servants have been busy, Lady. But if I were you, I would subject their reports to a closer study. Such who spy upon command often relate only what their mistress wishes most to hear."

"Perhaps, Lord Prince." She shot a sly, searching glance at Tallahassee, as if to judge the effect of her revelation.

If she expected to light a fire with that! After all, though the Prince had not uttered a denial of Idieze's malicious accusation, Tallahassee was scornful of any statement from that source. In fact she could imagine several reasons why Herihor might be on good and even confidential terms with a woman of the north through whom information affecting the border might flow. Did the Princess believe she dealt now with utter fools? When Tallahassee looked to the General Prince, she saw Jason, and Jason had had his secrets into which she had never thought to pry.

"The loose talk of servants has never been of interest to me. But your warning is now delivered. I have seen you, Idieze." Tallahassee deliberately used the dismissal for an inferior and was queerly glad to see the other's lips tighten into a grimace.

As she stood up, Idieze, too, was forced to rise, and by court custom she could not speak again. But as she withdrew, Tallahassee spoke swiftly to Herihor, hoping to convey by her very order her trust in him: "See that she is watched. Also I want her and her spying servants away from here as soon as possible. She came more to see than to warn, or so I think."

"She wears a mind-shield," Jayta said in a low voice. "It is not of her Talent. Also she would not dare speak of the affairs of the Temple, as she did, was this not a fact."

"But Zyhlarz—" Herihor protested.

"Yes, Zyhlarz, he who is Son-of-Apedemek in our time." Jayta's voice was strained. She stared after Idieze, already nearly lost in the shadows at the other end of the pool. "This is worse, far worse. Great Lady—we *must* know!"

"Herihor? . . ." Tallahassee made a question of his name.

"Be sure if there is any way possible, we *shall* know and soon. I have an officer with me—I left him in charge of the outer guard. He has undertaken such duties in the past; he will again. I have your permission to try?"

"You have my will on it!"

Then he was gone. Tallahassee put out her hand to the Priestess. "There is something else, there was a presence, one such as I felt in the other world . . ." Hurriedly she told of her experience before the arrival of Idieze.

"Yes, that can be the wraith of him who stole the Rod and the Key. He strove to follow you through the corri-

dor Ashake opened to reach your world. We have sealed
that. But that he has still the strength to follow you . . .
We shall set safeguards anew!"

It was late when Tallahassee finally went to bed. She
had had discussions with Jayta, later again with Herihor
who had sent his officer out. And the report came that
Idieze and those who followed her were safely pent in
their chambers, a guard set to watch.

As she stretched out on the bed, the faintly purring
kittens again beside her, she was so tired that she felt
wrung free of any emotion at all. Idieze had meant that
gossip concerning Herihor's barbarian woman to be
devastating. But then she could not know that Herihor
was—was like—Jason—a companion-brother—a . . .

There was a faint trouble born of that thought, but
she was too tired to strive to examine the source of her
uneasiness.

She roused at the growl of a kitten. Her room was
dark. Only a faint light shone around the edge of the
door curtain. Only—there was an intruder here. She did
not need the growling to know that someone stood beside her bed.

Tallahassee opened her mouth to shout for the guard.
There was a spray of liquid, stinging on her lips and in
her eyes, wet on her cheeks. She fell away, sick and
dizzy, into dark nothingness.

TALLAHASSEE was drowning, there was water about her and nothing to hold onto. Waves lapped over her head as she fought for air for her lungs. She was drowning! However, the waves were receding, though she could still feel them beat through her exhausted body. Not a sea—not water, yet she could feel movement and hear sound. The beat of an engine!

Her mind stirred sluggishly, but there was a spark of caution awakening, too. Recollection of what had happened came slowly. She had been in her bed and then—? The few moments of awareness, that spray in her face. . . .

She was certainly not in her bed now, nor in the villa. So where was she? Though she ought by this time, she thought, with a queer desire to laugh, to be accustomed to unbelievable changes of scene.

Though Tallahassee did not open her eyes (let whoever was near her believe she was still unconscious), she tensed her arms enough to know that they had been securely bound to her sides, her feet and legs immobilized in the same painstaking fashion. The bonds were not about her wrists or ankles, rather she was enveloped in some wrapping like a cocoon, though they had left her head free.

So, she was a prisoner and on a flyer. How they had gotten her away from the well-guarded villa was a question. Unless they (whoever they were) had methodically trotted about spraying all the guards and inhabitants with that handy little gadget they had used so efficiently on her. Idieze was behind them, she was sure of that. What utter fools they had been to even let her in.

When Tallahassee's thoughts drew upon the Ashake memory, she could find no hint that such an attack had ever been known before. Idieze had sat there and warned them. . . . Tallahassee's temper flared. She had dared—dared! Ashake memory burned at the thought she had dared to lay hands on one of the Blood! They would see what payment would be extracted for this outrage.

But who were "they" in this instance—beside Idieze, of course, and her servants? Userkof, probably, and beyond him, Khasti—that man of mystery. At the rise of that name in her mind Tallahassee knew a wariness that dampened but did not extinguish her anger. She must learn all she could.

First, she depended on her ears. There was the constant beat of the engines. She must be lying flat on the floor of the cabin, which she realized was very hard and unyielding. There must be a pilot, and . . . she tried to remember how many had accompanied Idieze. Two maids, she believed, and that crone of a nurse. But the wife of Userkof had never come without a squad of her own personal guard. Idieze would cling to that prestige no matter how supposedly private her visit.

None of the guard had showed up in the villa. Naturally not, the Amazons would not have allowed that. Even all of Herihor's men, save a single aide, had been restricted to the barracks beyond the landing strip. The villa was a house of women, as was correct for the unwed Daughter-of-the-Sun-in-Height.

There could be half a dozen enemies now about her, so the longer they thought her unconscious, and helpless, the better. Now that her ears had identified the sound of the engines she heard words, always pitched so that she could not quite catch them. Her sense of smell was an aid, too; she could pick up perfume—to her left—Idieze perhaps. And with that—yes, a whiff of that sickly sweetness from such a tube as the Princess had begun to smoke at the villa.

Farther away—another scent, vaguely unpleasant. But around her they were all very quiet. Perhaps this was how a mouse might feel trapped in a corner with a cat lazily on guard.

There had been a change in the flyer's rhythm, they were losing altitude, she thought, though she could not be sure. Then came a jar—landing. The engine cut off. Suddenly air puffed across her face, carrying not the freshness of the breeze at the villa, but rather a combination of odors that aroused the Tallahassee part of memory—that was like the tainted breeze of home— the smell of a city.

She was nudged in the side by someone walking past her. But no one came to lift her out—not yet. Very slowly she raised her eyelids a fraction. Her field of vision was very limited, but not so much so that she did not see a soldier in dull green. And in his hands—the case of the ROD!

She almost betrayed herself in that moment. What had they wrought at the villa to have that in their hold again? Could they have killed? She felt sick as she made herself face that thought. If they had reduced the others to impotency as easily as they had her, then it might well be that death had followed, leaving her entirely on her own in the hands of those who had little use for her.

Only one use in fact—that she alone in the absence of the Empress could handle the Rod. Did they have the Key also? She could guess that they would not overlook that. Within the wrappings that bound her she felt cold as she added up a sum and found the answer was probably complete disaster. What had she left for weapons? The memory—partial—of a dead girl, memory, but not the power that girl had commanded, and such courage and resourcefulness as were her own birthright. The Rod—she could hold it, she had proved that. But could she command what it symbolized? Tallahassee was not sure if that Ashake memory tape had been edited before it was forced upon her, but she believed that it had been. Naturally—they would do that for their own protection. What did Jayta know about Tallahassee Mitford that would lead the Priestess to allow her the full memory of her predecessor? Therefore she could not fight on Ashake's level, she could only bluff. And any bluff can be so easily called.

There was a tramp of feet again. Resolutely Tallahassee closed her eyes entirely. She was jerked upward, still lying prone. She must be on a stretcher as they did not touch her body. Now the stretcher dipped so she might have slid off, but there was a band about her waist on the outside of the wrappings to hold her steady.

Once more she peeked beneath three-quarter-closed lids: lights, and beyond them a scrap of night sky, also a back with wide shoulders, covered by a green uniform. Those vanished suddenly as the stretcher on which she lay was pushed into a dark, confined place. And she heard a noise like the slam of a door, whereupon all light vanished.

A motor started up, they were moving again. But there were no openings to give her any hints of where they might have brought her. Odd that she was making this part of the trip alone. Then something slid across the floor on which the stretcher so uncomfortably rested and banged against the side. Could that be the Rod box? With the inborn awe with which most of the empire regarded that artifact, Tallahassee did not believe that they would be comfortable with it close to them.

She tried to fit together the facts she had. There was no doubting she had been kidnapped, brazenly taken from her own home. And no one would have dared such action had the one giving the orders not believed he or she was invincible against any retaliation. The person of the Heir was sacred, even though in these latter years much of the ancient beliefs had worn thin enough.

To expect any help from Jayta or Herihor—no. Somehow it was very hard to believe that those who had taken her would leave any such strong opponents alive. So, she was on her own now, with only Ashake's edited memories to draw upon. However, what she felt at present was no longer fear, but Tallahassee's own temper on the boil. She had had to learn self-control early, yet her emotions were no less strong for that suppression. Now she must make the anger work for her as she had several times in the past, to bolster her own determination to succeed and uphold the courage to back that determination.

Idieze, Userkof, Khasti—She began methodically to summon to her mind all Ashake memories concerning those three. Userkof—he was perhaps the weak link. In a monarchy, which was firmly built on matriarchal inheritance, a king's son held little power. If he had wed Ashake—then he could have hoped for the crown. But he had never had a chance at that.

The Blood married by duty and not by choice, at

least their first and official marriages were arranged so,
though queens regnant had had their favorites, kings,
their concubines, often enough. And in this generation it
had been decided that fresh strains must be interbred,
with hope that the infusion would lead to a new generation with the Talent. The Empress Naldamak had been
married in her early youth to a very distant cousin who
had been killed two years later in the crash of a flyer.
And there had been no issue of that marriage, nor could
there be of another, for the physicians had pronounced
the Empress sterile. Thus furtherance of the line depended on Ashake—if she lived.

And if she did not live? Userkof—perhaps.

Idieze was only the daughter of a provincial governor
and had in addition a trace of overseas barbarian
blood—since her province was that of the sea coast
where the carefully supervised trade with outlanders
was conducted. That she would be empress in fact and
not just consort, should Userkof come to the throne,
Ashake had known for years.

Reluctantly she drew on the memory for Khasti. Here
were rulership and power, and sometimes one was not a
part of the other. One could choose to stand behind the
Emperor and wield through him true power. That was
what was suspected of Khasti. And it would seem that
suspicions were true.

If Naldamak returned at the Half-Year Feast, to appear enthroned in the ritual ceremonies of that time
without the Rod in her hands . . . that was what they
had tried to accomplish from the first. Now they had
both the Rod and Ashake! Or the seeming of that princess. From the memory she probed, Tallahassee discovered that Khasti was the least known, the most
suspected.

And what Idieze had reported—that the High Priest

Zyhlarz was imprisoned in his temple—was a forewarning that he could not be called upon. No, she had better depend only on herself, Tallahassee, rather than upon the infused memory from the dead or any aid from outside.

Though that was of little reassurance.

The vehicle in which she was a prisoner came to a halt. She closed her eyes. Ears only now. . .

She heard the clang of a latch at the back of the carrier. And then fresh air—this time a little less tainted with the effluence of a city—as the stretcher on which she lay was drawn out. Now she was being carried, and her bearers were in haste, moving at a trot. There was more light which she caught through the very narrow slit she allowed for sight.

"To the Red Chamber." For the first time she caught clear words. "And summon my Lord." That was Idieze speaking.

The Red Chamber? Yes, it was in the South Palace—that center which Herihor's men had been unable to penetrate—to which the suspected rebel leaders had been summoned. And that room had a gruesome enough history, for within it a hundred years ago, brother had slain brother in a battle for the throne and the hand of a half sister who had already chosen her consort.

Even the Talent had not kept the line free from the taint of ambition and greed. Perhaps that was why it ran so thin in this generation. Misused, or forced, that kind of power was lost. Perverted, it could turn upon the very one who tried to make it weapon or tool. Perhaps Idieze had chosen that shrine of infamy now with good reason. In such places, where emotion to a high degree had been released in some desperate and bloody action, there was wont to cling, even for generations, a residue of evil that could obstruct the clear sight of the

Talented, leave them open to an invasion that was to be feared above all things. Only she was not Ashake, so such an invasion need not be feared.

Her bearers turned a corner, then another. Finally the stretcher was set down, not on the floor, but apparently on a couch, for the surface gave a little under Tallahassee's weight. She heard them retreat, yet she was certain that she was not alone. And she strained her ears to catch the faintest sound.

"Ashake?" No "Great Lady" now. Idieze might have been addressing one in house bondage.

Close upon that call of name came a vicious, open-handed slap which Tallahassee had not been expecting. Without thinking she opened her eyes. Idieze leaned over her, smiling, her own eyes very wide and alive.

"I thought so," she observed. "Khasti said that the sleep-spray would not hold you too long. You have been trying to play a game, but the time is past for games, *Sister*." She stressed the last word. "You would never grant me that name, would you, Ashake? Nor stretch out your hand in any welcome. You 'saw me' when I came to you. Now I see you!"

Her lips parted in what was nearer a snarl than smile, showing small pointed teeth, very white against the red of her lips.

"I see you," she repeated, lingering over those words, as if from the saying of them she achieved some manner of contentment. "But will anyone continue to see you for long? Think on that, *Sister!*"

Tallahassee made her face as impassive as she could and gave no answer. Idieze's spite might be a weakness. And any weakness she must note and ready herself to use.

Idieze had turned and now approached a table as Tallahassee moved her head so she could watch. She had been right. The Rod had been brought with her. There lay the case in which she had placed it at Jayta's bidding. Idieze's fingers rested for a moment on the lid, but she made no effort to open it. She only looked back over her shoulder at her captive.

"You see—this too we have, in spite of all your struggles to keep it to hand. And very easy it was to take both you—and it. I have heard so much prating of the Power, the Talent. All my life people have been in awe of this thing, the force of which could not be proven. See how easy it was for us to defeat you?" She laughed. "I spoke of other roads, Sister—now we walk them. And there is nothing you can do to retrace time and change that, nothing!"

She ran her hand in a greedy gesture down the length of the case. Tallahassee thought that for all Idieze's spoken disdain for the Talent, she was still wary enough to let the Rod remain hidden; she was not so sure inwardly of the freedom of her other path as she would have the world believe. Tallahassee could sense the other's aching desire, the wish that it might be her own hand which could lift that symbol from its bed, that she need not work through Userkof.

Even as Tallahassee's mind pictured Ashake's cousin, so did he suddenly come into view. He lacked the height of Herihor and, though those two might have matched year-to-year in age, Userkof's flabby body and petulant expression seemed to add a toll of extra time. He did not wear a uniform, but rather loose trousers, fastened at the ankle, and a sleeveless over-jacket of white, much covered with elaborate embroidery. Also, his head was bare of the wig preferred by the court. Instead, he had a twist of flaming red scarf about his skull, which was a mistake, for it accented somehow the loose gaping of his thick lips, those jowls that softened and weakened his jawline.

"Maskaq said . . ."

Then his eyes went beyond Idieze and he saw Tallahassee. First they widened in what she could only believe was real surprise, then he laughed, a low chuckle.

"So you did it!"

Idieze was watching him closely, and Tallahassee did
not miss the shadow of contempt in her face as she answered:

"My Lord, did you then so doubt the success of our
plan?"

"There were many obstacles. She was in her own
palace—guarded," he answered. Now he advanced to
where Tallahassee lay and stared down at her before he
laughed again.

"Greetings, Cousin."

Idieze came to his side. "She does not answer. But she
will learn, will she not, my Lord?"

His tongue crept out, swept over his loose lower lip.
He might have been reaching into a dish that held some
sweetmeat he savored.

"Oh, yes, she will answer!" he agreed.

He reached out a thick-fingered hand and flicked Tallahassee's chin. There was something about him of a
small boy who had been dared to some act and must
carry through. Idieze must be full of triumph at this
moment, but Userkof, for all his seething malice and
spite, was still uncertain of success.

"My Lord." Idieze's hand on his arm drew him away
from their prisoner, back toward the table. "See what
lies here, ready for your hand!"

Her fingers went to the box and she loosened the
catches, throwing back the lid to display the Rod. The
pleased malice faded from her husband's face as he
looked down. Instead he drew a breath so deep even
Tallahassee could hear the faint hiss of it.

"It is yours, take it!" Idieze's expression held more

than a shadow of contempt now, which Userkof did not see. He was too intent upon the Rod.

"I have—have not the Talent . . ." he said, not as if he spoke to the eager woman, but rather as if he drew some warning from his own thoughts.

"Talent!" spat Idieze. "What need have you for that, my Lord! Has not Khasti given us and will give us yet again, much more force than these superstitious, meddling priests can conceive of controlling? You are of the Blood, you have only to pick up this, and you can command the Empire. Are you such a nothing"—her voice grew shriller, shrewish—"that you cannot do even this one small thing to gain a throne? You say you are a man, at least prove that in this much."

He had sucked in his bulbous lips, now he wiped his hands down the front of his jerkin as if they were wet and he might not be able to grip anything in them tightly enough.

"Khasti is coming." Idieze moved the Rod box a fraction closer to Userkof. "Meet him with the Rod. Do you now see what that will mean? He thinks too well of himself, even though *his* plan for getting this was a failure. You must make him understand that you are of the Blood."

Once more Userkof wiped his hands down his sides. He glanced uncertainly at Idieze, then back to the box and what it held.

"Show him," she hissed. "This you must do—or he will not be the tool we need. Rather will he think and plan for himself! He failed, but *we* have succeeded. Prove that to him, husband—and then you shall hold *him* in the hollow of your hand. For there must not be two minds and two wills when you come to power—only one!"

Yes, *yours,* Tallahasse thought. However much Idieze

urged, it would seem that Userkof was haunted by fear. As well he might be, Ashake's memory prompted. No one, not even of the Blood, could master the Rod unless there was that within them which answered to the undefinable thing that kept the ancient belief strong through all these centuries of study and testing.

Userkof put out one hand, and Tallahassee noted that it shook. How strong Idieze's will must be to bring him to such an action. She was not sure what the result might be, but that it would benefit Userkof—no.

Perhaps he had screwed up his small store of courage to its greatest point for he made a sudden grab with his right hand, wrapping his fingers about the staff a hands-breadth below the lion mask, snatching the Rod from the padded box.

For a single moment he held it before him, even as Tallahassee had done when the soldiers had broken into the ruin. Then—he screamed, high and shrill, more like a woman than a man. The Rod fell from his hold, struck against the floor and rolled.

But Userkof's hand—still held stiffly before him . . . The skin on his fingers was as red as if blood had been drawn. Slowly the flesh faded to an ashy grey. He screamed again as his fingers thinned into claws, fused so that he could not flex them.

Idieze shrank back, her face open for the first time to terror, staring at that horror of a hand, while Userkof's screams became peals of mindless agony. His wife nearly stumbled over the Rod, started to kick out at it, and then stopped, as if she feared now with a deathly terror any contact with the thing. Userkof sank to his knees, his body shaking. He still screamed even as he slid completely to the floor.

People burst into the room—guards first, their hand weapons drawn and ready. But when they saw what lay beside their master on the floor, looked at the ruin of his hand, they backed away. Their withdrawal cleared a path for another man.

Khasti!

He was as tall as Jason and spare of figure. His features were finer than Userkof's—he might well be a son of the Blood, though who he was remained an unsolved mystery. He could be traced no farther back than ten years when he had been discovered by a desert patrol beside a dead camel, himself barely alive. But he was of Empire stock and not a northern barbarian, and on his recovery he had managed to so impress the Commander of the fortress to which he had been taken that that officer sent him to New Napata with a recommendation to General Nemos.

From his first coming fortune seemed to have favored him. In spite of the fact that he made no close friends, nor confided in anyone, when he wished he could bind men to him. And no one denied the quick dexterity of his mind. Not even Zyhlarz could probe the extent of his intelligence. From the beginning of his life in New Napata, he shunned all that was of the Temple. Also, he allowed others in time to see that he disdained and held of small account what he deemed unprovable superstition, an attitude that attracted and soothed the egos of those who could not hope to ever enter the ruling center of the Empire.

Now he knelt beside Userkof, putting out his hand to clasp the wrist of that shriveled horror. Having given the claw fingers what seemed a single searching glance, he turned his attention to the man whose screams had died into a whimpering. Stooping, he stared straight into Userkof's distended eyes and murmured something so low-voiced that only the injured man might have heard. The rest of that company, including Idieze, kept well distant, as if the Prince was truly cursed, and that curse in turn might well envelope them all.

Userkof's eyelids slowly closed. Then his head rolled

limply to one side, his mouth slack, a thread of drool dripping from his open lips. Khasti took quick command.

"Take him to his chamber!" He snapped fingers at the guards who were very plainly loath to approach at all, but could not disobey. It was only when they bore the Prince from the room that Khasti looked about—at Idieze, at the Rod, and finally and most piercingly at Tallahassee.

There was nothing to be read in that stare he turned on her. And that very fact began to arouse within her the fear she thought she controlled. He showed no emotion, she could not guess at his thoughts. It was as if she were an object, not a living being. That quality in him was what Ashake had feared most in Khasti—now Tallahassee found it gripped her also.

So, PRINCESS . . . " Though he still looked to Tallahassee it was Idieze he addressed. "You have been busy, it would seem."

Perhaps that cool note of superiority that was plain in his voice snapped Idieze out of her state of shock. Her lips tightened as she drew herself up, once more self-controlled.

"We have succeeded," she returned. "There lies what your aide was sent to fetch and did not." With her foot rather than her hand she indicated the Rod.

"With what seems an unhappy result. My lord Prince has not managed to control it."

Khasti knelt on one knee again to inspect the Rod, bringing from the breast of his long grey robe something so small that he could conceal it in the palm of his hand. This he passed down the length of the staff, being careful, Tallahassee noted, not to come within touching distance. Twice he made that passage, up and down, and then opened his fist for an intent examination of a metal object no larger than the matchbox of her own time.

A single frown line deepened between his brows as he continued to study what he held.

"Radiation." The word he uttered was more for himself than his hearers. "But what? . . . "

Khasti gained his feet in a single lithe movement, came to Tallahassee's side with one stride. Now his hands loosed the bonds that had kept her captive.

"What would you do?" Idieze was beside him. "She—"

"It would seem, if all accounts are the truth," and this time his arrogant disdain of Idieze was very plain, "that the Princess Ashake can handle this symbol of might and show no harm therefrom. I would have proof of that here and now. Or would you, Princess, care to raise it from the floor?"

The last of her wrappings gone, Tallahassee sat up, only the thin night garment flimsy about her. She was stiff, and her back ached from her long imprisonment in one position. But she swung her feet to the floor, keeping her face as carefully blank as she could.

"Can you pick that up?" Khasti came directly to the point.

"I am of the Blood and the Upper Way," she returned obliquely. Tallahassee was not sure what method of control they might exert on her. But suppose she got the Rod in her hands, she might then be able to exert pressure on them in implied threat, though Ashake memory gave her only a very hazy and incomplete hint of how that symbol of authority was put into use.

"Do not! She will curse us and we shall die!" Idieze caught at his arm, dragged him back a little. "You have freed her—with the Rod in her hand you do not know what she can do!"

"She will do very little," Khasti returned calmly. "I will see to that. Now!"

In one hand he still held the object he had used to examine the Rod, but in the other he had, with the speed of a conjuror, produced something else, a glittering disk he spun out through the air, twirling it on the end of a chain. Against her will Tallahassee's eyes were drawn to that. Over her dropped the same compulsion that had held her to another's will back in the museum.

So compelled, she arose jerkily, not even mistress of her own body, and then stooped to close her hand on the Rod. The shaft felt warm, almost alive in her grasp. There was something she could do—should do—but Ashake memory was not strong enough to tell her. No, as Khasti's prisoner she must take up the Rod and carry it, three—four tottering steps forward, to place it once more within the guarding case.

"Well done, Great Lady." He made a sneer of her title as he leaned forward to push down the lid, seal the Rod from sight. "So it is true, you have some control over that thing." Now he swung the box up before her, holding it steady at her heart level and watching its surface. Once more the frown line appeared and he shook his head, perhaps denying the path of his own thoughts.

"You see, Princess," he said to Idieze, "how the new knowledge confronts and vanquishes the old? She is now as obedient to my control as might be a hunting leopard in leash."

"She is dangerous, too. She can be our deaths," Idieze retorted.

"Quite so. Yet it was you who brought her here, Princess."

"Because we must have a hostage until our plans are full ripe. They deem her the Heir, they will not want to lose her."

"So you have thought it all out?" Khasti smiled—coldly. "There is no need for the old methods of hostages and bargains. Did we not agree, Princess, that the time has come to sweep away the past and strike out anew, un-burdened by age-old superstition and custom?"

"We have not yet the strength—"

"We have all we need—for the present. If more must be sought, we know well where to discover it."

Idieze gazed at him in open bitterness. Maybe she was beginning to realize now, Tallahassee suspected, that the power behind the Emperor Userkof would not be his wife after all, but this other.

"Then what do we do with her?" She stabbed a finger at their prisoner as if she wished it were steel aimed to take the other's life.

"She will be very safe, Princess—with me." As he uttered those words Khasti let the whirling disk grow still, thrust it back into the folds of his robe. But before Tallahassee, released from that compulsion, could move to save herself, his hand came into the open again holding a cylinder. Once more there was discharged into her face the same narcotic spray that had brought her prisoner here. She remembered crumpling forward and that was all.

She roused slowly, but now she played no game of trying to confuse her captors concerning her state, for she had an idea that she could achieve nothing by that a second time. Around her shone light, bright enough to make her blink, and she heard queer sounds she found hard to identify.

The surface under her was level and hard as she levered herself up on her arms to look about. She was—caged! There was indeed a mesh of netting secured to four stout posts which kept her in one section of a very large chamber. But there was far more than her own cage here.

Tallahassee had no difficulty in identifying objects that would have been totally strange to Ashake. This was a laboratory of sorts, hardly differing from those in which she had once been a student. To her left stood a clicking box which reached nearly to the ceiling, but elsewhere there were two long tables crowded with retorts, bottles, instruments. And the air was slightly acrid with the fumes of chemicals.

On the nearest table there stood a much smaller cage, fashioned exactly like hers but of slightly different shape, and in that lay the Rod, out of its box again. Even in this strong light Tallahassee believed she saw a shimmer of radiance about the gem that was its head. Beside it lay something else—the Key—or at least an ankh which was enough like the one she had seen in Jayta's hand to be its twin. Yet it had not been displayed earlier as part of Idieze's loot.

There was something—a sudden small spark of Ashake memory stirred at the sight of it. But it faded quickly when Tallahassee tried to define it more clearly. She was left with the feeling that with the Rod and the Key together something could be done for her own defense and perhaps return attack against those responsible for bringing her here.

The cage did not have any visible door, and when she tentatively reached out her hand toward the mesh there was a warning reflex that made her wary of touching it. She would not sacrifice her single garment, but the cloth about her head might be used.

Carefully Tallahassee twisted it into a hard knot and then gingerly touched one end—holding it as far from her fingers as she could—to the screen wall. There came an instant flare as Tallahassee froze. What if her hand or arm had come in contact with that? Now she sat cross-legged in the middle of her cage and tried to see ahead—though the future was more than unpredictable.

Her thoughts were unpleasant and led nowhere, but it was some time before she began to realize that she was not alone in this room. Though she arose to her feet and turned slowly around, giving a long and searching survey to every portion of the long room, there was no one else. And the room itself was very open, with no screened corners or places she could not view.

But—she was *not* alone!

Some spy device? Tallahassee could well believe that such might be turned on her. Only she could not *sense* such a thing! That would be impossible. Therefore the identity was of another kind. Identity—yes, this was the same sensation she had had in her own—or Ashake's home—that there was a definite personality, unseen, perhaps unhearable (if it was trying to communicate), yet none the less present.

Slowly Tallahassee settled back on the floor of the cage. She was attempting something now that was very new to her. How does one locate a *thing* that is invisible (for this time there was not the least hint of the shadows she thought she had previously seen on such occasions) but which is *here?*

She set about methodically quartering the room, studying each part with a painful intensity, trying to "listen," if one might term it that, with her mind. Not there, nor there—nor there . . . Bit-by-bit she became somehow convinced that each judgment, ruling out a portion of the chamber, was correct.

In the end—she knew!

It hung close to the other cage, the cage where lay the Rod and the Key.

Who? Idieze had spoken of using her as a hostage, a term that presupposed there were those left who might bargain for her life. Naldamak, perhaps, on her return? The Followers of the Upper Way, locked now within their city temple? Or Jayta and Herihor? But had there not been that clean sweep of death at the villa which she had made herself halfway accept? She remembered that Khasti had pushed aside the suggestion of hostages as of little account. And this was Khasti's own stronghold—Tallahassee had no doubt of that at all.

They had sought always, those of the Upper Way, for things that might be termed of the spirit—for control over their own minds, the sharpening and lessoning of their own talents. Khasti was plainly one who was achieving, outside himself, something of their same ends. That he had succeeded in part was why she was here. Hypnotism, that must be the answer to that swinging disk that had compelled her to his will. Also there was the chemical which rendered one so speedily unconscious, as well the initial stealing and hiding of the Rod and the Key in another plane of consciousness, the one that was her own. What other weapons and tools had he devised?

It was still there, that *thing*. Now and again she tested her strange sense of awareness and always found the same answer. *Was* it the identity of the messenger who had wrought Khasti's will in transporting the Key and the Rod and then been "locked out" by Jayta's quick action in the desert? Could she communicate with *it* or *him*? Would she dare to try? Now that Khasti had the two symbols of power in his hold he might well free his messenger—or could he?

Tallahassee's hands balled into fists. There was so much she wanted to—had to—know. And all she could reach were guesses.

There came a sharp sound at the far end of the room. Here there were no hanging curtains such as she had seen at the villa, but rather a door of the kind she had known most of her life. Khasti, his long grey robe exchanged for a sleeveless, knee-long smock of white, came purposefully down the aisle between the two lengthy tables of equipment to face her.

He must have noted at once the burned edge of the

cloth knot which she had thrown down beside her, for now he smiled.

"You have already realized the folly of any thought of escape, you were quick," he commented. "How did you guess that there might lie some such danger in the walls about you?"

"I knew," she returned with all the calm she could command. "Just as," something made her add, "I know that we are not alone here now."

He looked around quickly, even a little startled, which displayed a small sense of unease in him that Tallahassee had not believed he would show. She marked it in her mind as a chink in his facade of complete authority.

Now he laughed. "Spirits of the air, Great Lady? Or the shadow of Apedemek Himself waxing strong to give freedom to His Chosen?"

"What is here, barbarian"—deliberately she gave to that word all the opprobrium it held among the nobility—"is not of Apedemek, nor of the Way, but of your dealing. It hangs now above the Things of Power." She pointed to the caged Rod and Key as if she could indeed see some shadow there. "It was sent by you, so it returns to you."

He had turned his head to look in the direction she had pointed. Once more he laughed.

"Do you seek to enweb *me* with your ancient follies? I know better than to believe such."

Tallahassee shrugged. "Believe or not, Khasti—but Akini is here." From whence had come that name into her mind? She could not have told, she had only said it aloud as if it had been that moment whispered into her ear—or called to her despairingly from a long, long distance.

His eyes swung back to her. "You know much, Great Lady. But it will do you no good to use the name of a dead man to make me believe in your 'Power.' Such a name could well be known already to those who have served your cause. I say that that cause is dead, just as you are dead when and if I will it so. Do you believe me? Yes, in the innermost part of you, you do. Good, now we understand each other. And I have yet to meet the man or woman who will not bargain for life itself.

"If you will give me your knowledge—such as how you blasted that weak fool Userkof without laying finger on him—of the energy that abides in this"—he waved to the caged Rod—"then we can deal together. Did you think that I would make any lasting compact with Userkof and that she-leopard who moves him about at her whim? They have been of use. Now they are no longer. One can wipe them away as dust from the hands."

"You want the Old Knowledge, yet you say it is no longer of any worth," Tallahassee returned. "It seems with your own speech you contradict yourself."

"Do I? Not so, Great Lady. That there is a portion of the unexplained, and perhaps the usable, in your knowledge, that I am willing to concede. Amun has endured a long time, and before that was Meroë, and earlier still Egypt. What you possess now must be only the near-worn-out crumbs of what was once a vast alien science. And there are other ways of achieving a return to that day—shorter and straighter ways. Let me learn the secret of such power as these can generate"—again he pointed to the smaller cage—"and there is nothing I cannot aspire to! Would you rise to set foot upon the very moon above us, Great Lady? Who knows that that might not be done!"

Though enthusiasm colored his voice, she sensed his falseness. This was how he wooed those dissatisfied with the past to join in his dream of the future. Did he think that one with the Talent could not read him for what he was—one who would rule, draw power into his hands, until he believed himself Lord of Life and Death?

The girl did not answer, only locked stares with him. One small part of her senses told her that whatever had brooded above the caged talismen now had drawn closer to him.

"Does Akini whisper in your ear, Khasti? He stands close enough now to lay hand upon your shoulder."

"So—you loose your witchcraft? Well, do not believe that it will do aught for you here. I have had secrets out of brains in plenty, Great Lady. Do not think that I will suffer yours to escape me. See—I shall give you but a small taste of what can be done."

He strode to the click box, pushed with his forefinger upon a certain place. Tallahassee jerked. It was as if a band had settled about her head, was closing, squeezing inward. Fear brought a sour taste to her mouth.

Then Ashake memory came without her tapping it. This is what he wishes, do thus and thus. All life is a state of mind, use your mind as a tool. . . .

It was as if she were able to retreat into herself, passing swiftly over some well-known path into a place of safety where no pain or fear could reach, a castle where the core of her identity could hold the walls against all assault.

She had believed that she could not find in Ashake memory those portions that dealt with the Power—yet this was such a one. Perhaps it was fear of that which had turned the proper key to let her in.

Thus—and thus—and thus!

She saw shadows, the very cage that held her became a wispy thing, like a cobweb, to be struck lazily away if such was her will. And Khasti—he was not a man, but rather a beam of light, pulsing a lurid red-purple, the color of arrogance and self-belief which no man should hold within himself. For all knowledge comes from the Fountain of Life, and such as Khasti deliberately deny that Fount and say it is naught.

There was a snap, a sharp return to the focus of normality. Khasti was himself again, standing by the machine, studying her with the frown line very deep carven between his eyes. Now he smiled, slowly, as had Idieze in her time, with the same tasting of a sweet that he would prolong to the utmost.

"So you are a little more perhaps than I had thought," he said. "Yet, in the end, we shall come to terms, my terms. And, because of your stubbornness, those terms will grow harsher the longer you withstand me."

He strode away, as if he had set her completely out of mind. Tallahassee drew a long breath and then another. But her attention was all for Khasti's back. Not because she feared his return or another attack, but because behind him, though he walked under the direct lighting of this place, which could support no shadow and did not, there trailed a tenuous *something* that she now could see. That which had kept watch above the Rod had now materialized farther, to cling to Khasti almost like a tattered cloak.

He paused at the far end of the room to bend over a table. Tallahassee thought she could see a sheet of paper laid there on which he was concentrating his gaze. The wraith hung about, seeming to nudge first one of the man's unyielding shoulders and then the other, striving to draw attention to itself, or so the girl believed. Yet Khasti displayed no sign that he knew of its presence. And the girl thought that that was the truth.

She waited for it to come drifting back to the cage of the Rod, as Khasti set aside the sheet of paper and now busied himself with the apparatus on the table. Instead it seemed to slip back into the air and was lost, nor could she sense its presence any longer. But she knew its name—Akini. And, knowing that, by the very ancient lore, she had a small bit of control over it, or would, if she remembered the proper ritual.

Now she was left to consider what had happened to her during that period of time when Khasti had striven to bring her to heel with his machine. He had failed in whatever purpose he had worked to gain. But she was still a prisoner, and so were the Rod and Key. Tallahassee did not expect any help from the outside to come thundering in to her rescue, even though she continued to doubt that Khasti had things as well under his control as he would have her believe.

There was one point he had openly made—that he was no longer, if he ever was, working to set up Userkof as Emperor. Tallahassee was not certain of the temper of the people. Would they accept a commander, a ruler not of the Blood? They appeared to have accepted the closure of the Temple, which was against all right and law and which once would have brought out a mob, squalling and fighting to get at the blasphemer who had ordered such a move.

He had offered to bargain with her, but more rightly he would in the end go straight to the source and bargain with Naldamak, the Empress. The woman who wore the triple crown was not now the same girl Ashake had called sister in the long ago. By deliberation, and through sorrow and loss, the woman in her had sunk so deep into the ruler that now she was forever remote and gave the impression of one who thought first of abstractions, and only last of human emotion, liking, hating, fearing.

Against such could Khasti use that strange weapon of hypnotism (for that surely was what the whirling disk was) and so make Naldamak his dupe? Then outwardly their world would continue the same, while inwardly he wrought a different life, overtaking the old.

Naldamak had been too set apart—Ashake memories had only the outward appearance, some guesses, to offer. This could indeed happen and very logically. Then why had Khasti suggested a bargain, attempted to force it on her—the Heir?

Because she was who she was. Naldamak had taken solemn oath she would not marry again, nor could she under the law now when her sterility had been judged complete. But with her Heir . . .

Tallahassee nodded. Even situated as she now was, she could find a wry smile for Idieze's fallen hopes. The wife of Userkof, instead of furthering her own cause, had played neatly into Khasti's hands by bringing the Heir within his reach. She wondered if Idieze realized that; certainly she was not stupid enough to believe that she could command her one-time ally any more.

Khasti poured greenish liquid from one beaker into another and brought it closer, to add the contents, drop by careful drop, to a bowl upon the table only a little beyond the cage of the Rod. There was a nasty smell, so irritating that Tallahassee coughed in spite of her efforts to remain quiet.

Having finished his task the man raised his head to look at her, as he picked up the bowl in one hand.

"Perhaps a chance"—he held the bowl up so she could not miss seeing it—"to forestall the imminent death of our dear Prince. A rather slim chance, I believe. But since I am called upon for miracles, so will I do my best. The Princess Idieze . . " He shook his head mockingly. "Alas, Great Lady, since she cannot call for your blood openly, I think she will try most energetically to obtain it in other and more hidden ways. Not because she loves her dear Lord, but because a crown she thought very firm, if invisible, upon her brow has been dashed away.

"Well, it is a hope. As for you, Great Lady, occupy

yourself with thoughts also—namely how long can even one who is Temple-trained lie pent without food or water. Food—maybe the longer. They say that those having the Talent are nourished rather than exhausted by fasting. But water is another thing."

And as if his words had been a key to open the door for the demands of her body, Tallahassee's tongue moved within a mouth that seemed suddenly parched. The mental image of water brought a terrible thirst to rack her.

THE THIRST induced by that suggestion from Khasti become a torment. Tallahassee rested her head upon her arms folded over her knees as she hunched in the cage. He had reached her once with the whirling disk that had put her under his command; had he done it more subtly again by words alone? She fought to control her thoughts—to shut away mind pictures of running water, of cups full and waiting for her to pick them up.

Did Khasti believe he could set her at the screen in a frenzy of thirst and so be rid of her? Drip—drip— A sound hammered at her control. Slowly she raised her head, peered at the laboratory beyond. There was a sink fashioned of heavy stone, fed by a pipe. And from that the liquid was falling drop by drop, though she had not noticed nor heard that before. Was this but a refinement of torture arranged by Khasti?

She closed her eyes again, tried to shut her ears to that sound, monotonous, somehow deadly to her control.

That Khasti had meant exactly what he said, she had no doubt. He would use her body to get at her mind. . .

Panic lashed at her. She covered her mouth swiftly with both hands lest she scream out in fear. That was his weapon—fear. But her defense was the anger she nurtured in herself as a wall against her own despair.

Drip—drip—

She shook her head wildly, as if by that gesture she could shut out the sound. But that was not the way to fight. Her best weapon lay in one place, of that she was sure, Ashake's memory. As she had done earlier she began to test, to draw on that knowledge, becoming more and more aware of the tatters in it—the blanks which, if filled, might have served her.

Ashake had gone through the long ordeals of the Temple, had learned there control of the natural processes of her own body that were only rumored as possible in Tallahassee's own world. Therefore somewhere there must lie an answer to this. . . .

The palms of her hands were wet with sweat as if the cage once more was heating around her, yet the mesh wires remained dull and fireless. She forced herself to breathe slowly, evenly. Thus—thus . . .

Again, it was as if she had broken through a wall, tapped a new reserve of strength she had not known existed. But—hold—do not be too quickly sure. As if she crept along some very slippery path with extinction waiting on either side, Tallahassee explored, to hold, finally to use, that bit of memory. The sensation of thirst receded. It was still there, yes, but it no longer made an unthinking creature of her.

She opened her eyes, tested her control by watching the drip of the pipe. For now—yes—she could hold!

But, the door beyond that pipe was opening slowly, as if by stealth. A moment later a figure slipped through, shut that portal quickly. Idieze hurried down the aisle between the tables, came to front the cage.

For a moment she only stood, surveying Tallahassee. However, this time there was no glint of malice in her eyes, no mocking smile to see her enemy so entrapped.

"Listen." She moved within touching distance of the wire netting. "You have powers. Even though that one has entrapped you, still he dares not put finger to that for himself." She pointed to the Rod. "He—he thinks to use *you* to accomplish his desire—"

"That being," Tallahassee commented dryly, "the rule of Amun for himself."

"Yes." Idieze's lips were tight against her teeth. "He says he will try to cure my Lord—I think he lies."

"And he has no more use for you?"

Idieze's expression became one of blazing fury. "This—this barbarian—and more than barbarian. He is not even human, not of this world! Oh, he thinks that is safely hidden, but there was the knowledge Zyhlarz gained. He came into this world through some demon-opened door. Where think you he learned this?" Her outflung hand indicated the laboratory.

"You were willing enough to accept his help, demon-inspired or not," Tallahassee pointed out.

Idieze laughed. "Why not? We thought then that he lived by our favor alone. We could expose him for what he was—something that had no right to live. He promised us—showed us . . ."

"Enough to make you believe, but not enough to warn you," Tallahassee continued for her. "It was his idea, was it not, to hide the Rod and Key out of time?"

Idieze brushed her hand across her forehead dis-lodging the set of her formal wig, but making no attempt to adjust it.

"Yes. But that did not serve, for you returned them.

Yet if he can open such a door once, it can be done again—and he can draw through those to serve him."

"You have not the mind of a child, Idieze, nor are you one whose thoughts have been emptied by the Greater Evil. Surely you knew that this would come of? . . . "

Idieze bit the knuckles of her clenched fist. Tallahassee wanted to laugh. Did Idieze think she could so deceive one with the Talent? (The Talent? queried another part of her mind which she did not take time to answer.) The woman's complete reversal of purpose was not to be trusted, of course. This was another ploy, probably set by Khasti for the purpose of weakening Tallahassee's own will. But if he believed that she could be won by such as this, what a very low estimate he must hold of her.

"He. . ." Idieze did not answer her question but switched to another track entirely. "He is not like other men, I tell you. He believes that all women are weak of will and purpose. He despises secretly our people because they will listen to women, be ruled by them!"

"Yet you believed he would listen to you, be controlled by you," Tallahassee pointed out. "So I ask again—why?"

"Because I did not know!" Her voice was shrill and high as if that question had in some way goaded her beyond endurance. "It was not until my Lord was struck down that he revealed himself truly—"

"You are contradicting yourself now. Have you not said that you had already learned he was not of our kind?"

"I do not know what I say!" Her hands, made into fists, were lifted as if to beat in the wire of the cage, perhaps reach Tallahassee. "We knew he was different, but not how different. He spoke to me—*me*—as if I were a barbarian slave. He—there was that in him which he had not dared show me before."

"Not dared—or not cared?" Tallahassee asked. "But

why come you now to me? You have seen me safely imprisoned by his device. What can I accomplish?"

Idieze shook her head from side to side. "I do not know. But you are learned of the Upper Way, surely there is something you can do."

"Perhaps. Reach out and bring me the Key and the Rod—" Tallahassee challenged her. "Then we shall see."

Idieze actually turned as if to catch up those talismen. Then she shrank back.

"If I touch what holds them, I die."

"So I have thought," Tallahassee commented dryly. "Thus you are caught in your own fine trap. But what of the others—those in the Temple? Have you appealed to Zyhlarz?"

"There is a guard on the temple—not of men—but of one of *his* things. No one has come forth for three days."

"And those who were my own guards—did you make them sleep and then cut their throats perhaps?" Tallahassee forced her voice to an even tone, just as she had forced control on her body.

"No!" Idieze stared at her. "To sleep, yes, when we took you. And maybe for a day thereafter. But they cannot come. Khasti has set his guards upon the city itself, so only those of his following may enter and none can leave. He waits to entrap the Empress so."

"So having safely taken New Napata he can do all—"

"No! There is one thing he cannot do!" Idieze interrupted. "He cannot take up the Rod. He tried it when it came into his hands before and failed. That was why he sought to hide it in a place he thought no other could reach. He cannot hold the Rod any more than could Userkof."

"You saw him try?" demanded Tallahassee.

"Yes. In his hand he held a box—so small a box. That he passed over the Rod and from it came a clicking, so that swiftly he snatched it away. But he had one who served him—whom he held by the strength of his eye and his will—and that one took the Rod—and vanished!"

"But that one did not suffer from the Rod?"

"Khasti put on his hands gloves that were very heavy. With those he gripped the Rod so no hurt came to him."

"He can banish the Rod again, can he not? And, if he can do many strange and wonderful things, can he not rule without it?"

Idieze stared at her now. "But you know whereof the Rod is made. It is the heart of our nation—our people! Without it we are finished. Why do you say that the Rod is naught and Khasti can rule without it?"

A bad mistake, Tallahassee realized instantly. Those of Amun were conditioned by the centuries to that belief. And if indeed the Rod were taken from them they would crumble as a state, die out as a people, because they believed this would be so.

"Yet he took and hid it," she pointed out.

"Only for a space was that to be. He had knowledge of where it lay—and only four knew that it was gone. Until you and Jayta divined it!"

"But you took it—and me."

Idieze pounded her fists together. "Userkof is of the Blood, none has denied it. The Empress does not wed, she has withdrawn much from the world. And you—you are of the Upper Path. What have you to do with ruling? Userkof was the Emperor's own son. Why should he not be ruler here?" Her words tripped over one another in a rush. "In other nations it is the king's own son who follows him—"

"Among the barbarians," Tallahassee pointed out. "Of them you have more intimate knowledge than do I. You speak of the Rod as being the heart of our nation.

Well, to it are wedded our own customs in turn. We do not follow barbarian ways."

"Throw my blood against me if you will! Yes, my grandmother was of the western sea people—but she was none the less for that. She was the daughter of a king—the which you are also."

So their suspicion of Idieze's blood mixture had been the truth. Not that that mattered to Tallahassee.

"What matters now whose blood runs in our veins? It is enough that Khasti has been turned loose to do his will. And since you know him better than do I, what do you propose then?" She brought them back to the main matter. And she indeed wished to have Idieze's answer to that.

When the other hesitated, Tallahassee asked another question. "How is this cage in which I sit controlled? I have learned there is energy in its sides so I cannot hope to batter my way out."

Idieze shook her head. "I do not know. I have been in this room only once before. And then Khasti said that death lay all around for the unwary and not to touch aught that was here."

"Then why did you come?" persisted Tallahassee. "To tell me how hopeless it is to struggle against this barbarian you sought to use as a tool, who now turns easily in your hand to threaten you?"

"I came because—because for all Khasti has said— the Talent *is*. And there is that in the Upper Way which is as powerful as his machines—to urge you to use that against him before it is too late!"

Tallahassee observed her through narrowed eyes. She had begun this interview by believing Idieze's arrival a subtle attack or feint against her, doubtless set in action by Khasti. But that new sense of hers was able to pick up now that the other was indeed afraid, that she might be quite close to meaning exactly what she said. Though of old the truth was not in this woman, now fear itself was forcing it out.

"I think you mean that—but it would seem too late," Tallahassee observed. "There is this you can do—alert those who would rise to crush Khasti, open a way for Jayta and Herihor—"

Idieze was already shaking her head. "I have told you—he has his own guards on Napata—"

"Guards can be—" began Tallahassee, when the other interrupted.

"Not these guards—for they are not men, as I said, but rather things he has wrought within *this* place. We know not how to command them, any more than I can release you from this cage. His ways are not ours."

"Perhaps not." Tallahassee eyed the block wherefrom came that steady clicking, where Khasti's adjustments had brought upon her that searing attempt to master her mind. "It is that"—she pointed—"that, I believe, controls this cage. What can you see on its fore?" The thing sat just at the wrong angle for her to be sure of the front panel.

Idieze moved to stand before it, her fingers laced behind her as if she dreaded above all else any contact with the thing.

"There is a panel; upon it burns a small red light. Below that is a row of buttons."

"How many buttons?"

"Four."

Four, and the farthest one controlled the agony with which Khasti had attacked her. Would any of the other three release her? It was a slim chance but Tallahassee dared not let it go.

"Do not touch the one that lies the farthest to your right. But try the one farthest to your left."

"It is death to touch. *He* said so!" Idieze made no move to lift her hand.

"If you did not come to aid me—then why?"

"Use your own powers," Idieze returned. "You of the Upper Way have in the past said that so much can be done in that fashion. I have given you warning, but I will not touch this thing born out of demon knowledge."

Then she wheeled and ran, as if she were pursued by some horror. Tallahassee watched her go. Use her own powers indeed. Was Idieze really moved by panic, or had all her talk been a deception, a need for knowing *what* Tallahassee, with the vaunted Talent, could do? Her conviction that the other had been truthful in her fear was shaken. Truth and falsehood could be skillfully mingled so that one could not be sifted free of the other.

But she was haunted by those four buttons. If she could only have talked Idieze into trying them! She stared at the block to her left as if by will alone she could manipulate its secret, win her freedom.

Will alone! Ashake memory responded with another fragment. Unluckily one on which she could build nothing. She only knew that Ashake herself had once witnessed such a feat of telekinesis. But it had been performed by several adepts acting together, joining their powers. And it was not common.

She closed her eyes, to shut out the here and now, to better catch any hint from that second and mutilated memory. Some details were so clear that she could believe she herself had done such things. Others—they blurred, faded, when she tried to fasten on them. An animal could be mind-touched, brought into control, made to perform any task within its physical ability. But such manipulation of other life forms was not to be indulged in. For all life was to be respected and man should make no slave of any species. Also, where in this room was she to find anything she could influence, even if she might have the power to do so?

Where . . .

Tallahassee grew tense. That—that presence—for which the name Akini stood—it was back. She opened her eyes and looked to the cage of the Rod above which it again hovered.

But—Akini—it—was not alone!

She could see nothing, only sense that there was more than one presence here now. Still she watched, hardly daring to draw a deep breath.

"Akini . . " Tallahassee moistened her lips, spoke the name aloud.

There fell a queer kind of stillness—as if what she had not seen had halted, was listening intently, that now these presences were focusing on her.

"Akini." Again she spoke the name, this time was a certainty that she was heard.

There was a flow of emotion, striking her suddenly as a wave might batter a cliff—anger, fear—but not aimed toward her. No, that emotion flooded out for her to receive merely because she was present and in some way had established a thread of contact with the identity that generated it.

But the contact seemed all on one side. If it—Akini—knew her or *did* respond as she thought was happening, he—it—could not reply.

Save that there was a wavering in the air, a shadow, a wraith—like a cloudy outline with a blob for a head, stick arms, legs, a cylinder body. . . . It writhed, as if striving to set what might be suggestions of feet on the floor, still it wavered and floated. Save that somehow it could control its movements enough to front her cage.

Emotion again—a pleading—a voiceless cry for help.

"Akini." She summoned up all her control, for the

wavering thing held for her a growing horror, and she had to force herself to look at it. "I am a prisoner—I cannot help you—*now*."

Did it—he—understand? There was plainly a struggle to hold to even the slight visibility it had. And then one of those stick arms began to stretch, pulling into itself the gossamer material of which the whole was fashioned, until there swam in the air restless coils of what might have been a great serpent—very thin in diameter but long. It looped about the cage from which Tallahassee watched it wide-eyed. She had been able to accept in part the wraith she had first seen, but this was something else again, and still it was spinning out its substance, refining it down and down to threadlike size dimensions.

The thread end poised before the screen of the cage. Tallahassee threw up her hands before her face. She knew what would happen. It strove now to enter between the wires of the deadly mesh! To reach her! Her control snapped. With a cry she sank down, her face against her knees, her arms laced protectingly over her head—though there was no protection, she was certain that could hold against what hunted her now.

There came a touch, cold, sending a tingle up her arm from the wrist where it had met her flesh. She tried to ball herself more closely together, moaning softly, with no thought now but the need for escape.

Then—it was gone!

Tallahassee need not look up, out into the laboratory, to know that. Its snuffing-out was a mental not a physical thing. For the moment she was only thankful for its withdrawal, for her escape—though what she feared from it she could not have said.

There came the sound of a closing door. Idieze returning? She above all must not see Tallahassee reduced to these straits. The girl fought for control of her shivering body, of her scattered, half-dazed thoughts, and drew on the dregs of her energy to raise her head.

"How is it with you, Great Lady?"

Tallahassee's blurred sight cleared. Khasti! But at this moment Khasti, though he had entrapped her, was safe compared to what had hung in the air, tried to reach her through the netting of her prison walls.

"Do you wish to drink?" he asked with malicious mockery, crossing from the side of the cage to the sink to twist the end of the dripping pipe. A gush of water answered him.

"Water, Great Lady. At this moment I would say you would find this sweeter to the taste than the rarest of wines. Is that not so? . . ."

She shook her head, not so much in denial, as rather to clear her thoughts. Khasti was a man, that other thing . . . She shivered.

"No water? They have trained you well." He turned from the pipe flow and began to swing the disk once more on its glittering chain. But this time she was forewarned and closed her eyes. He could not hypnotize her a second time.

"Stupid female!"

"Was Akini stupid too?" she asked.

"Akini! Where got you that name? Your spies have been busy." There was a new harshness in his voice. By the sound of it, he had moved away from the sink, was coming closer to the cage.

It was as if a hand were laid warningly over her lips. For a second out of time that other was here again. There was anger—toward Khasti—a sharp hint of silence for her.

"As yours must have been in their turn," she answered. But she did not open her eyes, even though she believed she could no longer hear the thin swish of the chain passing through the air.

"It does not matter." He was master of himself once again. "You might wish to know, since he is your kin. Userkof did not 'depart for the west'—as your people so euphemistically put it. He will live—a cripple—and no more thankful to you for that than any man would be. As for you, I leave you to your dreams, Great Lady— and I do not think that this night they will be pleasant ones!"

She could hear the scrape of his sandals on the floor. He had passed her cage, was going to that block bearing the buttons. Another assault upon her mind? She was too worn now—she could not hold—she could not. . . .

Did she, or did she not catch the faint click of a button? There was a hum, soft but persistent, walling her in, as if the wires of the mesh were being plucked as might be the strings of a harp—singing—lulling . . . Her head fell forward once more so that her forehead rested on her knees. She tried to prod her will into keeping her awake, but she could not. . . .

There was no cage—instead she walked down a corridor and she knew what lay at the end. This was the trial of a novice who must face death and then rebirth or never tread the Upper Way. Fear walked at her shoulder, matching step to step with her, but she did not turn her head to see what form it took. She fought to breathe evenly, slowly, as one does when fully relaxed, to make each pace as measured as the next. Behind her lay years of the Temple training, before her only this last ordeal, and then she could prove her right to the Power which she felt struggling now within her, seeking the outlet that only the initiate could truly give.

There hung the dark curtain of death-in-life and beyond it was life-in-death to be fronted. Ashake held high her head as if she already wore the initiate's crown of victory. Her hand moved, closed upon the curtain and drew it aside. With the courage of a warrior she stepped out into the deep dark.

THIS was her last trial. By years of training, or learning to know herself and the depths of her thoughts even when they were unpleasant to face, she had been prepared for this moment, to be pitted against the fears from which those thoughts were born. For none can wield the Power until they can command themselves fully.

She was ready. . . .

But something else struggled in her. Not her fear, no. This was urgent, a warning. Ashake hesitated within that all-enveloping dark, tried to understand.

This—this she had done before! She was being made to relive the past by some force outside herself. And that force had only one reason, that through her it could learn secrets which none who knew them must ever reveal.

What was truth, what was a dream? Was this a false warning sent to her as a test? She had no real knowledge of what an initiate faced, save that it would try her to the

145

utmost. And was the beginning of such a test the suggestion that it was not the truth but a lie?

She raised her hands to her head, knew that they were
shaking with the tension building in her.

Truth—lie? Which, oh, which?

Panic—she must not panic! She was Ashake of the
Blood, one destined since birth to walk this path. Therefore, the truth must be tested by the one way she had
been taught. She disciplined her mind, forced away the
panic, sought those guides that should stand ready at her
call.

They were clear as she pictured them. But, they were
not there! Once more she tried. There was nothing, nothing at all, nor could she sense that in-gathering of Power
which should have drawn about her.

So, this was not as it should be. But—what had
happened? She swayed as she stood, fighting the force
that would have moved her on—that coercion came from
without, was not born of her own will!

She was Ashake. Who dared play such a perilous game
with one of the Blood? Who dared challenge the Rod and
the Key?

She was Ashake . . . she was . . . she was . . .

Identity itself blurred. Ashake? No, then who? She
thought she moaned, and yet did not hear her cry ring
through this utter dark.

She *was* Ashake! She must be, for if she set aside
Ashake—then there would be a stranger, and one could
not live as a stranger. No, this assault was part of something that sought to spy, through her, on the secrets of the
Upper Way. And with that answer, a steadiness spread
through her giddy mind. Who dared use her so? There
was only one—Khasti!

As if his name in her mind shattered some spell, the
dark, the ritual hallway disappeared. She stood now in the

open under the hot sun of the northern desert. Before her lay the battered walls of the oldest shrine. She hurried (or seemed to skim the ground as if she flew rather than touched foot to the sand and grit) toward that.

Here was the temple, battered by time and by the ancient enemies, yet still it stood. Apedemek, whom the ignorant claimed she and her clan worshipped, yet whose great statue stood as only a reminder of something else that could never be caught and held in any stone, no matter how skillful the artist, stood facing her.

The blind eyes stared out above her head, the hands grasping Rod and Key were above her too. Yet the talismen were not stone. They glowed with life, pulsed with force. She had only to reach out and grasp them. Then all that was of the dark would not dare to contain her. Up she reached, straining farther and farther, yet her fingertips could not even touch the end of the Rod. Furiously she struggled, knowing in her mind just how the power of the Rod must be wedded to the power of the Key by the initiate and what would come of such a mating.

She was Ashake, she alone had the right to touch the things of the Past. Within her the Power swelled, as she knowingly drew upon it, for it would seem that as she used it in her need, so did it grow and flow. She was Ashake.

Now the shrine wavered before her eyes as if it were a painting on fabric. Vast rents appeared from side to side. It tore and was gone, leaving her facing—nothing, an emptiness—that strove to invade her mind, wash free all she knew, even her own identity. No!

She drew upon the Power, pulled it about her as one might pull a cloak against the force of a storm. The emptiness could not reach her. For she was Ashake.

She saw that emptiness in turn break, not tear slowly,

as had the shrine, but shatter in an instant. Objects faced her. She was neither in the hall of the temple, nor in the northern desert, she was—

The cage!

And beyond that barrier, Khasti watched her narrow-eyed.

Tallahassee was a little dazed. Still she knew what he had tried to do to her. He would have learned the sacred, the forbidden, by making her relive her initiation in a dream. That he could have sent her so far as he had into the past was frightening—but she had won!

"You are stronger than I thought," he said slowly. "But not too strong. This time I took you to the threshold, the next you shall step across it. Let thirst and hunger weaken your body, and you cannot so well hold out against me."

She made him no answer. Why should she? He stated the terms of their struggle and those she must face.

"I wonder . . ." he continued musingly. "There is something in you that I do not yet understand, and it is not born of your nature. For this thing registers in spite of your stubbornness. Listen well, Great Lady, I have resources beyond any you can comprehend in this world—"

For the first time she spoke then. "This world? Are you then of another world, Khasti?"

He frowned. Perhaps he had made a mistake. If he had, he decided quickly it did not matter, for he answered her.

"There are worlds upon worlds, Great Lady. Does not your own 'learning' "—and he made of that word a sneer—"hint at such?"

"We all know there are worlds beyond. Look upon the stars which are suns. Many of those warm worlds we cannot see," she returned calmly. But she was inwardly uncertain, he was getting too close, too close to Tallahassee, who had slept while Ashake had fought her dream battle, but she was now awake.

"Your legends," Khasti continued thoughtfully. "What say they of such worlds, Great Lady?"

Ashake shrugged. "Why ask me, Khasti? You must have made yourself familiar with those long ago. Would you tell me now that you come from such a world? Do you expect me to look upon you as a god because you might have knowledge such as we have not? Knowledge varies, it is of many kinds, comes from different sources. Yours is built on what lies about us in this room. It is not ours, nor would any man of our kin be fitted to use it. Therefore, I can believe that it may be unearthly—"

His frown had deepened as he looked at her.

"Such a thought does not alarm you then?"

"Why should it?" she returned. "Did you believe that I would say you were a demon as might those unlearned? There is that in you which is not kin—nor are you like anything we have heard of among the barbarians. Thus you must have come from a place we know not, the proof being that you stand here and now to meddle dangerously in our affairs." Again she shrugged.

"Meddle dangerously in your affairs." He caught up her phrase. "Yes, that is how you would see it, I suppose. But what if I have much to offer you—"

"No merchant offers trade upon the point of a sword," she snapped and was pleased to see the answering flash from his eyes. Ah, she had indeed pricked him then. "You want not a bargain with us, you want the Empire. For what reason I do not know yet, unless there is such a boiling of desire to rule within you that you must seize all you can, as a greedy beggar stuffs his mouth with both hands and then reaches quickly for more. Why are you now so frank with me, Khasti? Is it because you have not broken me as quickly as you thought to do? Is there some time limit on your meddling?"

He was silent and she knew a small surge of triumph. If that guess were only right! What time limit, and set by whom, and for what purpose? She had the questions, but who would give her the answers? For she believed in this exchange she had brought more out of him than any other in Amun knew.

She had angered him, but she did not care.

"For a female you are quick with words, bold words—"

"Among your kin then, Khasti, are those of my sex considered the lesser? That is a barbarian belief. I hear that their women in the north are wed to become the possessions of the men. With us it is not so. Does that anger you a little?"

"It angers me not at all. It merely amazes me that your men are such spiritless fools as to allow such a way of life to continue," he said coldly, in spite of the anger she sensed in him. "It is well known that the female mind is inferior—"

"Inferior to what, Khasti?" She had the last word with that, for he did not answer, but turned and strode away. She waited until the door closed behind him, alert to any other move he might make toward the box. It had been the force of the box that had drawn her to the brink of remembering her initiation, thus almost supplying him with some knowledge he pried for.

She was alone once more. He had left the water trickling from the pipe in the sink. Her mouth was dry. Now also her stomach begun to proclaim its emptiness. She folded both arms across it, hugging herself, as if by touch alone she could persuade herself that she was not hungry.

If she could only have talked Idieze into trying that row of buttons. One of the four *must* release the cage. She remained sealed here at Khasti's pleasure. She tried to occupy her mind with the hints he had dropped. *Was* he really from off-world? Ashake memory had produced some very ancient tales of "Sky Lords" of incredible learning who had visited Khem of the Two Lands thousands of years ago. Tallahassee's memory was ready to babble less intelligently of flying saucers, and the speculations concerning ancient spacemen giving impetus to the beginnings of civilization in that time and world.

Or could Khasti have slipped through another rift in spacetime such as had entrapped her, merely stepped from another world like this, but one that had followed a different pattern of history? It did not really matter—he was not only here, but well prepared to engraft on Amun his own pattern of living.

She was thirsty! The trickling of the water . . . And she was empty enough to feel weak. How long could she stand up to this? She could not even be sure how long she had been here. That period of induced unconsciousness might have been prolonged past her judgment of time. How long could she last?

Her headache came from the strong light as well as lack of food. And it would seem that her brave fight against the demands of her body was nearly lost. Once more she rested her forehead on arms crossed over her upheld knees. She was very close to the sleep of complete exhaustion.

There was a cold touch on one elbow, a tingling that spread from that point of contact up her arm. She had felt something like that before. Her mind seemed sluggish. What? . . .

She made herself look up. This time her extra sense had been too dulled to alert her. Outside the cage coiled that serpent thing, and it had again inserted a tendril to make contact with her.

Even her fear arose slowly, and she could not make the effort to avoid the thing. It clung to her flesh. And now it seemed no longer so wispy, so tenuous. In dull horror,

Tallahassee watched the thread turn milky and opaque. At the same time she realized that it was drawing strength from her in some way. Down that thread traveled the opaque suggestion of new solidity. She reached out her other hand desperately trying to break its hold on her. But she could not. It remained, sucking, sucking.

Tallahassee began to cry weakly. For all her brave words to Khasti, her struggle to remain herself, this she could not fight any longer. She was too worn from the earlier struggle to defend herself.

She crumpled on the floor, moaning a little. Still the thing fed—if you could call this vampire-draining feeding. Then, before she blacked out entirely, it loosed hold. Wonderingly, she saw something else appear in the air before that shimmer, which she identified with Akini. It was milky white and it was a hand. A hand that ended at the wrist. Its fingers were now being flexed as if about to be put to use.

Her mouth open a little in astonishment, Tallahassee pulled herself up on her knees. The hand was moving away from her, propelled through the air as if it had been given some task it must do. The outline kept changing, as if to hold it in shape was almost too great a task.

But it was before the cabinet now—nearing the row of buttons. Another dream? Perhaps one evoked by Khasti to further torment her and drain her obstinate strength so that he could make her wholly his tool?

The hand darted forward. She could not see from her cage just what it had done. But certainly there was no change in the wire mesh about her and, for a moment, she knew a deep disappointment. If the hand thing had not intended to kill, she had hoped a little that it might be here to help. Only—nothing had happened. She was as securely pent as ever.

While the hand was fading, the strange stuff of which it was formed sloughed away from the shape of fingers into wisps. It was moving again, shapeless though it was, not back toward her cage, but rather to the near table. For a moment, as long as it took for her to blink twice, it hung above the smaller cage that imprisoned the Rod and Key.

Could it be? . . .

Tallahassee's heart lurched within her. Perhaps she was not free—as yet—but that other . . . She watched the shifting blob, which the hand had melted into, pass through the mesh of the smaller cage, make a dart at the Rod and as swiftly recoil, not only recoil but become dispersed into nothingness.

There was a feeling of shock in the air. Akini was gone, driven away by the very force he—it—had attempted to use. But what had he done at the control box? Perhaps turned off whatever unseen defensive mechanism Khasti had set up to protect what had been stolen?

Ashake—Ashake knew what could be done. If Tallahassee surrendered completely to Ashake there might be a chance. But if she so surrendered could she ever regain herself?

Only—now she believed that even such a loss as that was worth a chance to escape. She closed her eyes, summoned Ashake memory defiantly, opened her mind to what the other had to give.

Ashake crouched down. Her body was feeble, it was true, but she could still draw upon some inner energy, enough, she prayed, to do what must be done. She fixed her stare on the jeweled head of the Rod.

"Come to me!" she commanded with all the strength left at her command. "Come to me!"

Slowly the Rod arose from the surface on which it lay, the lighter end sloping upward ahead of the heavy, begemmed top. Now it was pointing upward at a sharp angle, the tip aimed at the woven wires of its cage.

"Come to me!"

The tip touched the cage mesh. There was no reaction. Sweat streamed down Ashake's face, lay wet in her armpits, on the palms of her hands.

"Come to me!"

The tip of the Rod exerted more and more force against the cage. Ashake fought to give it all she had in her. Then the cage tilted, fell to one side with a clatter. And, since it was bottomless, the Rod was free. It whirled around and swooped through the air, aiming straight at Ashake as she called it.

Like a lance it struck the side of her own cage. There was a brilliant flare, which made her cry out as the backlash of radiance struck her. But she had had time to shield her eyes. When she dared to look again she saw that the Rod lay on the floor. But where it had dashed against the cage there was a black patch in which holes appeared to spread. The metal was rotting swiftly as might a broken fungus.

Now she looked beyond that growing hole to the Key and raised a hand weakly.

"Come!" she called for the fifth time.

The Key arose, slower and more sluggishly, since she called now from the very dregs of her failing strength. But it obeyed her, moving in jerks through the air and settling at last in the trembling palm she held out to it.

The hole in the screen was open enough to let her through. And at the touch of the Key new strength flowed into her. She crawled out into the open, stooped to pick up the Rod, and then, with *her* weapons in hand, stood to her full height and looked around.

Such a use of the Power had set up a troubling in the whole atmosphere. If there were any within this building who possessed a scrap of the Talent, they would be warned. She waited, using the force renewed in her from the talismen of her people, to listen, not with her ears, but her mind.

She could pick up no instant response to the waves of energy she had projected. But she owed a debt, whether the other had meant to save her or had only been working to liberate the Rod. And debts, for one of those who walked the Upper Ways, lay heavy.

"Akini?" With mind, not voice, she sought the creature who had come to her rescue. She did not know what he wanted with Rod or Key. But manifestly it was *not* to put them in Khasti's hands, for all that labor had been to free them.

But there was only mind-silence. When Akini had striven to reach the Rod had he—it—been blasted forth to extinction? Somehow Ashake did not believe it.

She tottered toward the sink with its trickle of water from the pipe. Gathering both Rod and Key into a single hand, she held the other under that less-than-finger-wide stream. It filled the hollow of her palm, and she brought the liquid to her lips, sucking carefully, doing this many times until her thirst was at last quenched.

Hunger was still with her but that must wait until she could find food. Purposefully now she started for the door, waveringly at first because of weakness, but each moment that she held the precious talismen it decreased a little, so at last she walked with much of her old, determined stride.

There seemed to be no catch or knob on this inner side. Well, she could use more of the charge of the Rod to burn her way through. But that she would rather not do. She did not want to further deplete its energy.

However, when she set flat palm to the door, its surface shifted slightly so that she inched it forward, listening all the while, hardly daring to breathe lest that faint sound cloud her hearing.

Now that the crack was wide enough, she could see a slice of darkness beyond. After waiting a very long moment more to make sure there was no sound at all, she slipped through.

There was darkness facing her and not too far away, but both Key and Rod radiated light enough for her to see that she was now in a narrow hallway that ran into deeper darkness both left and right beyond the range of the talismen's glow.

She had two choices and no guide as to where each might lead. Not only was there no sound, but, Ashake decided, there was a queer emptiness here, as if all that which made life as she knew it had been barred.

Left—right . . . Her head turned as she quested for some guide as to which way would lead her back to the world she knew. Finally she faced right, holding the Rod and Key before her to give the best light possible, and started on.

THERE was no other break in the wall after she left the door of the laboratory. Also the hall narrowed. The way was very dark and there was a queer heaviness in the air. She might be approaching some very ancient tomb which the living had not troubled for a long time. Then the hall ended abruptly in a flight of stairs that led down into a thicker dark, far beyond any radiance of the Rod or Key to pierce.

So she had chosen wrongly. Her path should have been left rather than right. Could she retrace her steps, or might her escape be already discovered?

Tallahassee was deeply tired, in spite of the energy she drew from the talismen. Her hunger was an additional weakness. To go on down into this dark was folly. Back. . . .

Somehow she inched around, looked back. Now a sound reached her. Footfalls, echoing from sandaled feet, where her own bare ones made no noise. There came a flare of light—though it was very small and far away. Someone had flung wide open the door of the laboratory. She was cut off, with only the dark descent left as a way of escape. Khasti!

Her heart beat faster. What strange weapons he could command she had no way of guessing. That he would pursue her, Tallahassee had no doubt at all. But there was one thing. . . .

Steadying her hands with all the control she could summon, she turned fully to face that distant door, raising Key and Rod. She moved them through the air, drawing invisible lines of force, while she recited under her breath the Words of Power. Let him come then. He would meet with something that might not entangle his body, but would strike at his mind, alien though it might be.

Then, with foreboding, she began the descent. The hall above had felt dry and chill, but as she went carefully from step to step downwards, the chill became damp. The air about her, in spite of that odd dead quality, held a touch of moisture.

New Napata was on a river. Did this warren run down close to those sites where the river had been long ago covered over and hidden? She listened, both for an outcry from behind, and for any sound below. What she had done to seal this way in her own defense had drawn from the store of energy in the Rod and Key. Now their radiance was faded, did little more than light a single step ahead. Smells assaulted her nostrils—of wet, or rot, of nauseous things she could not set name to. Still the steps descended into the heart of a dead-black pit. Who had wrought this way and what use it had been in the past she could not imagine. At least it had been unknown to Ashake before.

On the steps led, down and down. Tallahassee was so tired she trembled from head to foot. Only her will kept her mind clear. Clear enough to—

She halted, her feet together on a step slimed with moisture, and raised her head high.

"Akini?" There was a presence here again. No, more than one! They were pressing in against her, as wayfarers in a desolate land might press inward to warm their hands by a camp fire. And what drew them were the talismen!

She was right, one of those was Akini. But who were the others? If she could only communicate, discover what they wanted, for their emotion touched her mind, grew in her thoughts. They were avid. As her own bodily hunger gnawed at her, so did some greater hunger tear at them—a hunger that was centered in what she bore. They did not even seem to be aware of her, only of what she carried.

"Akini!" Again she tried to reach that one presence she could put name to.

"Give—us—the—life. . . ."

Only a flutter of thought, so faint and far away that she could barely pick it up.

The life? Did the Rod and the Key mean life to these wisps of identity?

"Life!" The word was no stronger this time, but more imperative.

Ashake took firmer hold on the talismen. It seemed to her that the presences were trying to clutch at what she held, drag them from her grasp. But they were too weak to achieve that.

She took a deep breath and then made her answer: "Guide me hence, if you can—and I, who use the Power, will also try to give you life!" Could she bargain with these lost things? And if she did strike such a bargain, then how might she fulfill her part of it? She did not know. But there were Zyhlarz, Jayta—the others of the Upper Way—surely among them all they could give these wraiths either life or eternal peace.

That weak plucking at the talismen quieted. But they were not gone. She took heart from that. Perhaps they had understood. If they were creatures of this darkness, they surely knew the ways below.

"Akini?" She made a question of that thought.

There was a touch on her wrist. She started and glanced down. A threadlike tendril rested there. And through it came a thought.

"Forward."

She could only trust in this. If it were a true bargain, she had won. But, since there was no turning back, she must accept what came. Down and down she went. The Akini presence was there, the others too, but they had withdrawn a little, trailing behind her.

They reached the foot of the stair and stood in a place of evil smells and air so thick that she gasped as she went. But she did not have to travel far. On the wall to her right that thread, which had touched her wrist, centered on a block of stone that the radiance showed faintly.

Ashake held closer the Key and the Rod. Here was the line of an ancient arch, but it was filled with blocks of stone, wedged in to seal what once opened there. Ashake raised the Rod, willed its power higher. She tapped with its tip against the top stone, and as she did so she muttered the old chant of the Builders. This she had never done before. She was not even sure that she knew all the words that released such power. And in the days when the Builders had wrought with the Talent, then there had been a number together wielding their wills into a single strong force.

But the stone was moving. Slowly Ashake drew the Rod back toward her, and the stone followed, to fall at her feet. So much force expended to loose a single stone! Could she achieve the withdrawal of another? She was not sure, but once more she lifted the Rod and whispered the chant. And once more a stone obeyed the summons of her Talent.

Three more blocks were so dislodged. She could not do it again! As she stood she wavered on her feet, her eyes blurred. But there was a hole—large enough to crawl through? It would have to be!

Her single flimsy garment was torn, there were bleeding gouges in her skin, grazes on her arms and legs which burned. But she had won through, to stand in yet another dark way. But this lacked the dampness of that other, and there was now a current of air blowing about her, enough to hearten her.

Ashake limped forward on bruised and bleeding feet, weaving from side to side of that narrow way, until first one shoulder and then the other scraped painfully along the stone. But the straight path was very short. Again she faced steps, very narrow steps, leading up into the dark.

She pulled herself up from one to the next. All the world had narrowed for her to that one rough staircase. And she was not aware, until she came upon it, of a landing some four steps wide. In the wall to her right, a little below her eye level so she had to stoop a fraction to gaze through it, was a peephole from which came a wan light. She could see only a small fraction of what lay beyond, but it was enough to both startle and encourage her. For she gazed into the inner courtyard upon which fronted Naldamak's own suite in the Inner Palace!

There was no sign of a door here, and anyway she had no wish to come blindly into the open—not until she knew more about the situation that might face her. Up again . . .

Tallahassee did not count the steps, but here was another landing. No, it was the end of the stair itself. And when she peered through another hole it was into the dark, as if this hole was covered. Taking Key and Rod both into one hand, she felt along the wall before her. Surely there lay some way of opening it!

Her fingers dropped into a hollow in the stone, which was barely perceptible, even when she held the talismen close to it. And it was her sagging weight as she leaned forward that must have released the hidden catch.

Ashake tumbled out through a narrow opening, to become entangled in a hanging which she nearly ripped from its high wall fastenings as she fell. Her head and shoulders lay on the carpet of the room she had entered so secretly, and the smell of delicate perfume, the freshness of good air filled her nostrils, cleansed her lungs of the foulness filling those dark ways below.

She was so spent that she did not even try to move for a space. Khasti himself could have stood before her at this moment and she would not have been able to summon the strength to face him.

It was a frightened cry that brought back her wits. She lifted herself a little, with one arm braced under her, and looked up hazily into a face she knew.

"Sela—"

"Great Lady! But where—"

"Sela," she forced out the name again with her remaining strength. "None—must—find—me. . . ."

Naldamak's old nurse—would she, or could she, understand?

"No—one—Sela . . . The—Candace is in danger. . . . No—one—must—find—me. . . ."

"Great Lady, none shall." It was an old voice, thin, and weak, but there was the same decision in it Ashake had always heard. "Lady, I cannot carry you; can you walk?"

The words were very far away. Ashake fought to get to her knees.

"Hungry—so hungry. . . . No—one—must—know. . . ."

The Key and the Rod—they lay where she had dropped them on her fall. Now she drew them to her.

"Sela," she said to the woman bending over her. "A cloth—for the precious things. They must be hidden!"

"Yes, Great Lady." There was a soothing in that voice. The age-hunched figure was gone and back again, before Ashake could move, over her arm a long strip of finely embroidered stuff, the cover from a table. She knelt stiffly before Ashake and spread it out, sitting back then on her heels as the girl, making slow work of it, rolled the talismen into a tight bundle.

"Sela—where? . . ."

"Great Lady, trust me—safe they shall be!" Sela had gotten to her feet and into her outstretched hands Ashake thankfully surrendered her trust. If there was one faithful soul in all of New Napata, it was Sela for whom Naldamak was and always had been the whole world.

Ashake did not remember how she came into the bed. But when she awoke it was dark in the room save for a distant lamp. And beside that Sela sat on a stool, nodding.

"Sela." Her own voice was hardly more than a hoarse whisper but it brought the nurse hurrying to her side.

"Lady, Lady," she patted Ashake's shoulder where a dressing of soft ointment was spread to take some of the sting out of the graze that had burned there. "Do you remember now?"

"Remember?"

"You talked so wild, and words I did not know. All the time I fed you the soup and wine—and you did not seem to recognize me. And your poor arms, your legs. Lady, what happened to you?"

"I was a prisoner—for a while." She had spoken words Sela did not know . . . that other part of her memory began to stir. She was Ashake—no, she was someone else. Who? Tallahassee! So that part of her was not forever buried as she feared that it might be.

"The Candace?"

Sela's face wore an expression of worry. "Great Lady —they will tell me nothing! And since you came I have stayed within these walls. There is a maid servant—she is new come since you lived in Napata—but she is of my home village and her I can trust. It is she who brought us food. And she says that there is talk that the Candace has been—lost! Over the desert when a storm arose. This is whispered widely in the city. But"—she raised her chin defiantly—"I will not believe it. My dear Lady— she is wiser, very wise. And she has good reason to watch even shadows. Also she had with her the Sworn to Sword—twelve of them—though they went disguised in the dress of lady-in-waiting or maidservant. Think you such would let *her* come to harm? I do not think she was lost in any storm, rather that she hopes her enemies will believe that. But you—Great Lady—what happened to you whom we thought were safe at Gizan?"

Tallahassee gave an edited version of what had happened since she had been kidnapped from the villa. Sela drew in her breath with a hiss.

"That there is a secret way now open to this room! That is evil, Great Lady. But you have brought the Precious Things safe out of danger and when the Candace returns—then there will be an accounting!" She nodded her head vigorously enough to send the edge of her sphinx headdress flapping.

"This maid of whom you speak—" Tallahassee sat up in bed. Her sore and bruised body protested every movement so that she felt she, for one, was not in her present state prepared to take on battle with anyone—let alone an enemy as strong as Khasti. "Can she find a way to reach the villa. I do not know whether Jayta and Herihor still live—"

"They do, Great Lady. You slept for two days and three nights—you seemed to drowse even when I brought food and fed you. So you do not know. The Prince General holds the northern roads, all of them. He summoned his own regiments of command and four others which are loyal and to be trusted. I think he strives to keep open a path for the Candace. And the Daughter-of-Apedemek has come before the walls of Napata and formally demanded entrance—she was seen by many. But the Temple—it is shut by some vile sorcery of this demon from the desert, and none has seen or heard of those who were so locked within.

"The Prince Userkof is said to be suffering from a fever, so his Lady commands in his household. And no man or woman knows where Khasti hides himself or what mischief he plots." Sela sounded out of breath as she finished that rush of words.

"Can a message be sent to the Prince General?"

"Great Lady, there is some strange wizardry set upon the gates. They stand open but no one can pass through. And the people are greatly afraid of this thing. But—Lady—there is something . . ." Sela twisted her robe in both hands. "I saw this for my own self when I went upon the outer balcony watching for the Candace—to see if perhaps her flyer comes."

"What is it?"

"That man cannot pass whatever barrier the vile one has put there at the gates, but animals may. It was a fruit seller's donkey that broke from its master as he argued with the guard. And it passed beyond the gates as if there was nothing there but the empty air we see. But when the master would run after it he could not follow. And the donkey went on down the road."

"An animal can break through." Tallahassee considered the point. "And a bird?"

"Those in the garden fly high," Sela answered. "But how can an animal serve your purpose, Great Lady?"

Pigeons could—if this was her own time, Tallahassee thought, and she had a convenient coop of trained ones. But a wandering donkey, even a horse, who might stray through the gate could not be a reliable messenger. It was a silly and baseless idea, yet her mind clung to it.

Had she been able to reach the Temple, she believed that there would have been no problem. There were a few trained in the Talent who could travel outside their bodies—visit other places. Such a one could reach Jayta and pass a message, for their training was aimed in part toward such encounters. Unless Khasti had foreseen that also and erected some barrier such as the cage he had imprisoned her in until the wraith—

The wraith—Akini!

She turned to Sela. "Sela, you know much of the palace and all those who dwell within it. Have you ever heard the name Akini?"

It was if she had reached out her fist to thump the attendance gong.

"Akini! Great Lady—what do you know of Akini? Does not his mother come daily to sit in the outer court waiting for him? She has wept until she has no more tears in her, but still she will not believe that he has gone without a word to her. He was fan bearer to the Prince Userkof and between two days he was gone! None know where—only his mother will not believe that he went off with the barbarian—"

"The barbarian? What barbarian?"

"He was one who came to New Napata with a message for the Candace, but she had already gone north. By our laws, as you know, he could not stay past three sunsets. But the Prince Userkof received him, and it is said that the barbarian took a liking to Akini and offered him good payment to return to the coast, speaking for him with those peoples through whose land he must go. But the mother swears that Akini had no intention of doing such a thing, and she has petitioned that Candace's officers find what has become of her son."

"This barbarian—what manner of man was he?"

"Great Lady, as you know, the northern barbarians are not like us—they have hair of different colors and their skins are very light. But this man was different yet again. He might have been one of the Old Ones out of Khem, for he looked akin to those ancient statues which are kept in the Palace of Far Memory. He spoke our language badly, and ever he looked about him as if he found all to be strange indeed."

"Did he seek out Khasti?"

"Not so, Great Lady. And as you know he was directly under the eyes of the Sworn Swords while he was in New Napata, for barbarians do not roam our cities freely. No, he wanted the Candace, and when he asked for whoever ruled in her place that *one*"—Tallahassee knew Sela referred to Idieze—"sent him word that her husband was of the Blood. But whether he knew that he was not dealing with the truth or not, I do not know. They had but one formal audience and did not meet again. So, at last the barbarian left . . ."

Another Khasti? They had all they needed with the one they had, Tallahassee thought ruefully. So Akini—he had been real—a person Sela had knowledge of. But what was Akini now? And how had he been so altered, or entrapped, as to exist only as a wraith, a troubling of air? It was Khasti's doing, of that she was sure. If she could only reach Zyhlarz, for even Ashake memory could not supply the answer to such a riddle as this.

There remained the other question—how might she contact Jayta and Herihor, reassure them that the talismen were out of enemy hands and safe? Animals could go out, but, undirected, what could animals then do? Undirected—she began to consider that. Dogs were noted at running down masters at a distance, nosing out nearly extinguished trails. Cats had been known in her own time and world to cover long distances to be reunited with families who had moved away, or had lost them from cars during trips.

Herihor, as became his rank, had a dwelling in New Napata, but he was seldom there. Certainly not enough to keep a pet animal. But . . . She must think—plan— on a single small and very wild chance.

"Sela, who is at the Prince General's dwelling now. Can you find out?"

"I can find out, though it may take a little time, Great Lady—there are but few I can trust here. However, there is one of the Sworn Swords who had the fever and is now well. Her, I helped to nurse. I can bring her to you, and she will be better able perhaps to discover what occurs in the city. But first, Great Lady, I urge you to eat. You are very weak and your body is so worn that you look as if *you* have had the fever!"

"Well enough."

Sela apologized that the food she brought was mainly cold but the maid could only smuggle a portion of regular food on the tray supposedly intended for Sela herself, who added dried dates, cheese, small loaves of bread which she could conceal about her person.

Sela had helped Tallahassee into one of the Candace's plainer robes, settling a folded linen headress over her cropped hair. But looking in the mirror the girl was forced to admit that she did resemble one recovering from an accident. She still felt thirsty and drank deeply of the fruit juice and water Sela brought her. But at least she was ready to face this Amazon guard of Naldamak's, on whom her plan, hazy as it still was, depended so much.

When Sela brought the young warrior to her room later that night Tallahassee still wondered if one could do such thing.

"Great Lady!" The wonder in the newcomer's eyes was clear, but her salute was instant. And Ashake memory recognized her for a girl recruited on one of the northern royal holdings, her family loyal for generations to the thone.

"Greetings, Moniga. These are dark times." She went abruptly into what she would say.

"True, Great Lady. You have some mission for me?" The other girl was intelligent and also came directly to the point.

"Is it possible for you to get into the dwelling of the Prince General Herihor, there locate some object which has been close to his body. A piece of clothing he has worn that has not been washed—though that may be impossible. If not, something he has handled and not too long ago?"

"Great Lady, to his place I can go. Whether I can get what you wish—that is another matter. But be sure that I shall try."

"There is something else—if you get this thing that will bear the scent of the Prince General, then do you also bring to me Assar from the hound kennels."

"Lady, it has been said, so will it be done." The Amazon saluted and slipped carefully through the door Sela held open for her.

"Now—" Tallahassee turned to the nurse. "A pen I need, and ink and paper—these should be in the Candace's study."

"They are so—but I shall bring them Great Lady. Stir not forth from this room. There has been seen in the upper corridors a maid from the Prince Userkof's wing. She has no good explanation for why she wandered so."

Involuntarily Tallahassee glanced at the wall where

hung the tapestry covering the secret way. Sela smiled a little, though her expression was still worried.

"None will come that way, Great Lady, not without giving good notice of their coming. I have set a certain alarm, one the Candace herself uses by her other door on occasion when she wants no disturbance. You may rest easy for that much."

But could she, Tallahassee wondered? How long would the protection she had woven in that pit hold back Khasti if he sought her there? She must be alert constantly, and her attention swung from the wall tapestry to the chest in which she had seen Sela lay the bundled Key and Rod.

$\mathcal{T}$ALLAHASSEE spread the sheet of thick paper on a corner of her "sister's" dressing table, and fingered the pen absently. For a moment she was frightened. She could pen her message in her own words—but that would be unreadable. Ashake's memory must provide again, so she opened the door once more for that. Characters slipped so slowly into her memory she had to fold and tear away the paper where she had made too many mistakes in translating the message she hoped, just hoped, could reach Herihor wherever he now might be. It was such a gamble that she dared not build upon success.

With infinite care she wrote out the characters of a running script that had developed from the long ago hieroglyphics of the north.

"Safe—Ashake; also—Precious things. City sealed. Candace—be warned."

She read it over twice to be sure that she had made no

errors in transcription. Then she folded it into a small square and looked to Sela.

"I would have a piece of cloth about so big"—she measured it off with her hands—"and it must be golden in color. Also, there is needed a length of the stoutest thread you can find, with a needle."

The old woman asked no questions but went straightway to one of the chests of robes and began turning out its contents. Among them was a cloak to which Tallahassee pointed.

"That is the very shade!"

Sela shook out the garment. It was embroidered heavily along the hem but the upper portion was bare, and from that she ruthlessly cut the cloth Tallahassee had asked for. It was a very tough silk and, as the girl pulled it this way and that to test it, she saw that it was very tightly woven. Into the square she folded the note, making a packet that could have been hidden in the palm of her hand. Sela had gone out, but swiftly returned with an ivory spindle round which was wound linen thread as tough as any cord, with a needle already strung upon it.

Now it only remained to see if Moniga could fulfill her part of the task—and how long it would take to do so. Tallahassee could no longer sit still. In spite of the pain from her bandaged feet, she paced up and down the chamber, keeping well away from the curtained windows along one wall. Even though those gave only on a garden which was private to the Candace, and the light within the room was very limited, she wanted none to guess the suite was occupied.

"Sela—" She looked to the woman who had gone back to her stool in the corner. "What of the Temple? Has aught changed concerning the Son-of-Apedemek and his priests?"

"No, Great Lady. Only . . ." Sela paused and lowered her eyes.

"Only what, Sela?"

"Great Lady—there are whispers in the city—even those who serve the Daughter of Amun repeat them. They say that the Son-of-Apedemek may already be dead and with him all those who follow the Upper Way—that they were killed because they summoned demons who turned upon them."

"Rumor can cause much trouble, Sela. There is no weapon in the end as difficult to overcome as the tongue of an enemy."

She must get out of here, even if she could not leave the city. At the moment she felt as if she were again caged, if not as tightly as when under Khasti's power, yet nearly as helplessly.

"Sela, this maid of whom you spoke—can you bring her to me?"

"Great Lady, at this hour she is lodged with the maids in the sleeping room where they lie six together. To summon her would cause remarks."

"Can you get for me a garment such as she wears in her daytime service?"

"Great Lady—" Sela started up from her stool and came to stand before Tallahassee. She was a short woman and had plainly once been plump. Now the flesh hung loosely on her arms and her plumpness had centered in her belly. Her face was a network of fine wrinkles so that her kohl-encircled eyes had a strange look, almost as if they were set in a nearly naked skull. But she carried herself with the authority of one of importance in the household, and now a fraction of that authority rang in her voice:

"Great Lady, what is in your mind now to do?"

"I must be free of this room. You cannot continue to hide me here in secret for long, Sela."

"There is no need perhaps to hide, Great Lady. Call

forth the Sworn Swords. With them before your door what man can reach you?"

"Khasti—or those of his following can," Tallahassee returned grimly. "Did he not have me out of the villa, with my own guard at the doors? He has more tricks than a camel carries fleas upon its mangy skin. And we do not know what force he controls even now. Zyhlarz, himself, and the others could never lock the gates of New Napata as this stranger from nowhere has done. No, he may believe me here, but perhaps before he can move as openly as he must to reach these rooms I shall be gone."

She crossed to stand before the wide mirror on the dressing table.

"I am tall," she frowned at her reflection, "and that I cannot conceal." Ashake memory reminded her that this height was something that was a part of the inheritance of the Blood. "For the rest, yes, I think it can be managed. Get me such garments, Sela, as a maid wears."

The old nurse hesitated. "Great Lady, I pray you, think of this again. What will you do, where do you go?"

"That I cannot answer, because I do not yet know. But I will not do anything rashly, so do I swear to you, Sela."

The other shook her head, but she went. Tallahassee sat down on the bench before the dressing table. Her face had none of the cosmetic coating now. She peered a little more closely, advancing her face closer to the surface of the glass. As limited as the light was cut off by the curtains, she could not be mistaken. That stain which they had put upon her body when she had assumed the part of Ashake was beginning to fade a little. Certainly she looked paler now than she had when she had last looked upon herself back at the villa.

But to ask Sela for the use of . . . no! She had no intention of adding to her difficulties by allowing a woman so devoted to the Candace to realize she was not in truth the Queen's sister. Wait—she had seen maids at the villa who were much darker of skin even than Jayta, Herihor, or the two priestesses. She could certainly use that for a basis for her request to the old nurse. Tallahassee was pleased with herself at that bit of reasoning.

She began to open the jars and boxes ranged neatly before the mirror, peering into them. Some held fragrant oils, the perfume of which, concentrated by being so lidded, arose headily in the air. There was the familiar eye paint, and two jars of delicately scented creams, a little bottle of red which might be liquid rouge or else lip paint. But most of this would not be worn by any maid.

Her head turned sharply. Unlike the curtains that had veiled the doorways at the villa, the entrance to the Candace's personal suite had a door fitted for complete privacy. And in the stillness of the night she had caught a scratching noise.

Tallahassee stole as noiselessly as she might across the outer room. Then she heard a sound that reassured her—a whine. Moniga must have succeeded!

But Tallahassee was still cautious as she opened the door. The Amazon stood there, and, held on a tight leash, was Assar.

"In!" The girl waved them on, shutting the door instantly. Assar whined again, head high, sniffing. Of all the Saluki hounds in the kennel, he was the best for coursing, the most intelligent of his very ancient breed. He needed both talents now, and perhaps a third, to be receptive to orders given in a way even Ashake had never tried. Those of the Temple had worked in this fashion with cats, great and small, since the breed had always been sacred to Apedemek. But a cat hunted by sight, and only one of the highly trained palace hounds could course a scent over a long distance.

"You have it?"

"This, Great Lady." The Amazon produced one of

those broad ceremonial wrist bracelets that had evolved from the bow guards of the ancient archers. It was interlined with a padding of leather.

"His Highness sent it to the city a month ago, for the stone of the setting"—Moniga pointed to a large carved carnelian—"was loose. There was nothing else that he had recently worn."

"It must do. You have been both quick and clever, Moniga."

"The Great One desires, her desire is the law," the Amazon replied formally, but her face shone.

"Assar—good Assar." Tallahassee rested her hand on the dog's head. His smooth coat was golden, soft and silky. On the ears, legs, and tail, it feathered long and gracefully.

The tail swung at her greeting and he followed her into the bedroom where she reached for the small packet she had made ready. As she sewed it to his collar Assar stood patiently, looking up into her face, now and then whining very softly as if asking what was to be done.

She had chosen the color well, the packet against his throat could hardly be distinguished from his own coloring. Now she took up the arm band Moniga had brought, turning it so that keen nose could sniff at the padding where, if she would have any luck at all in this mad venture, Herihor's scent would linger.

Tallahassee allowed the hound some moments to make sure of the scent, and then she knelt before him, so that they were nearer eye to eye, and put one hand on either side of his high-held head. Now—she willed into her mind a picture of Herihor, then of the way north, again of Herihor. Patiently she kept herself to the task, repeating it a dozen times over. The worst was not being sure whether she was reaching that brain so alien to her own, whether Assar knew what must be done. But she was coming once more to the end of her own power of concentration. She would have to accept, now, either success or failure.

Getting somewhat stiffly to her feet, Tallahassee held out the leash to the Amazon.

"There is the small gate of Nefhor—How late is the hour?"

"It is within two hours of dawn, Great Lady."

"So. This you must do, Moniga, and without being seen if possible. Loose Assar near the gate. If he goes through, then we have a small chance of reaching the Prince General. If I have failed, doubtless he will return with you. But take every precaution you can not to be observed."

"There is the guard of the Prince Userkof at the gate, but they are not alert." The Amazon wrinkled her nose expressively with scorn. "They believe that the barrier is complete."

"Still—go with care."

"That we shall, Great Lady." The Amazon saluted, and Tallahassee let dog and woman out of the door. She sighed and went wearily into the bedroom, to collapse once more on the bed, where she lay staring up at the painted ceiling, her restless thoughts not allowing her any peace.

"Great Lady." Sela had slipped in with her accustomed skill at appearing by the bedside before one was even aware she was there. "You must rest—or the fever will come. I know not what you plan to do, but you cannot attempt it yet."

Her wrinkled hand gently touched Tallahassee's forehead, and it seemed to the girl that the coolness of her fingers spread swiftly throughout her tense body, relaxing nerves and muscles.

"Drink, Lady."

Before she could move, a practiced arm slid beneath her head, raising her up until a goblet met her lips. She drank, her weariness overcoming the need for action for the moment.

"Sleep . . ." Sela's hand stroked her forehead, peace and safety in that gentle and loving gesture. There had been so much—so much . . .

"Sleep . . ."

Tallahassee's eyes closed as if the lids were so weighted she might never hope to raise them again. And if she dreamed, no memory of those dreams carried over into her awakening.

Sunlight edged the window curtains when she roused. And the room held heat—the fans would not be at work with the Candace gone, of course. She felt the moisture in her armpits and gathering along her temples, under her breasts. After blinking for a breath or two, she sat up in bed and reached for the tall glass bottle set on the bedside table, tipping a goodly amount of the water it held into its attendant glass and drinking it down. Sela's stool in the corner was vacant. There was no sound through the hot and airless rooms of the suite.

Piled nearby upon one of the chairs was white clothing. But first of all she wanted to bathe, to rid her body, if only momentarily, of the sheen of sweat and gain what refreshment she could from cool water against her skin.

Bundling the clothing under one arm (it was the servant's dress she had asked Sela for) Tallahassee went into the luxury of the Candace's bathroom where water from one lion-headed pipe fed into a basin in which one could sit nearly awash to the shoulders, and then lapped out an overflow slit in the wall. She dug her hands deep into a sweet-smelling cream that lathered and washed away like soap. But her skin *was* lighter—several shades lighter.

How good was Sela's eyesight? Had age dimmed it any? Discovery might depend on that alone now. She rinsed and wiped herself down with one of the towels hanging on a nearby rack. Then she dressed in the narrow white dress which was very close to that of the priestess, save that the bands across the shoulders were not white but red and there was no girdle to confine it at the waist.

"Great Lady—" That was Sela hurrying in.

"Listen." Tallahassee was occupied with her own problem, hoping to so avert Sela's notice of the color change in her skin. "If I am to pass as a maid, Sela, I should be darker of skin. Have you aught to use to make me so?"

Sela's hands were close-clasped together. Now she twisted them as if afraid.

"Lady—they have come." She seemed not to have heard Tallahassee's question.

Herihor? Jayta? Dared she believe that?

"Who have come?" She fought her own rising excitement. Sela's appearance did not suggest that any help had arrived. Instead, there was alarm in the wrinkled old face.

"Four of the greater Nomarchs, Great Lady. They have been summoned to council, yet the Candace is not here. In the Prince's name they have come because they are told that naught has been heard from our Lady for two days, and ill must have come to her from the desert storm! Great Lady, if this be true . . ." She was trembling so that Tallahassee set her arm about the bowed shoulders, led Sela to a chair and pushed her down upon it. Going to her own knees she caught the shaking hands in her own and spoke very gently.

"Dear Sela, if our Lady were dead—would I not know it? I have the Talent and so has she in some measure. Do we not then feel death when it opens the Far Gate for those we love? I swear to you that this has not happened. Be sure that the Prince General is using his forces along the border to find Naldamak and no men have more knowledge of those lands.

"But tell me, which of the Nomarchs have come to New Napata at such a false summoning?"

Sela's tear-filled eyes held hers.

"It is true, Great Lady—she has not Gone Beyond?"

"Would I not have told you, Sela, you who have loved and served her all her life long—who held her to your breast when she was but an hour old? You have been her mother-in-life. It is to you I would have first spoken had I such ill fortune to know."

"She is my Sun-in-Full, my dearest heart—"

"That I know well, Sela—"

"When she was little I was her guard and her comforter, when she became the Candace she paid me honor, putting me first in her personal service, even though I was old and sometimes forgetful. Never has she spoken a cross word to me, Lady. And now—now they say she is dead!"

"But since she is not, we must prevent any such word spreading before they hold council on it. Which Nomarchs, Sela?"

Sela gave a last small sob. "He—he of the Elephant, and of the River Horse—"

"Both of the south," Ashake memory supplied, "and those that rebelled a hundred years ago."

"And the Leopard, the Ibex—"

"Of the west where the barbarians trade. I see. But the Lion, the Cheeta, the Baboon—they come not? North against south—west against east."

"Great Lady, the Elephant has many mighty warriors. When they arose under Chaka in the old days there was much killing before the Beloved-of-Apedemek—the Pharoah Unie who was then—restored law in the land. And there is talk of new barbarian weapons—"

"Yes. And so we must know of what they plan. Do they dare to meet in the Great Chamber of Council?"

"It is so."

"Well, there are secrets of the Candace that are not known even to as close kin as Userkof." Tallahassee arose. "There will be a listener whom they do not suspect. This, Sela, is what you must do. I will have to go to a certain place and not be marked during the going. Can you get me that with which to darken my skin so that I look like a maid from the south?"

Sela seemed recovered from her first fear. With her head a little to one side she regarded Tallahassee who hoped her own uneasiness did not show. Then the old nurse smiled.

"I think that may be done, Great Lady. The Lady Idieze—you may not know it, but it is true that barbarian blood is hers. She is as pale as the belly of a fish by nature. She allows not even her lord to ever see her so. There is an oil she keeps in secret, only it is not as secret as she thinks. And now that she makes ready to welcome the Nomarchs there will be no one in her inner chamber. It shall be yours to use."

"Do not take any risk, Sela."

"Risk, Great Lady? Has not the Candace given me the power of overseeing all her household? If I check upon the willingness of the maids, and how well their work is done—then I am only about my lawful business." She laughed and Tallahassee echoed her.

"Sela, you are a very wise woman—"

"Great Lady, had I had the tending of *you,* instead of your being sent to the Temple for the raising, you would know how much one can learn hereabouts by merely listening and saying little."

When the nurse had gone again, Tallahassee sat down and allowed Ashake memory once more to enter her conscious mind. Ashake could recall the day when the last Pharoah had taken Naldamak and her (she being on one of her visits from the Temple school)) along a certain corridor and showed them a secret that only Ruler and Heir might know. They had sworn an oath of silence that day. But she would not be breaking it now, for that secret was designed as an aid in just such a situation as this.

This council had been called in Userkof's name. Did the provincial rulers summoned here believe that she, Ashake, was dead also? Or was it they were merely ripe once more for rebellion, a rebellion perhaps financed and armed either by Khasti or by some of the western barbarians who had always resented their treatment by Amun, the refusal of the Empire to treat or ally with their quarrels, for they were a divided number of peoples forever at each other's throats in one political and military struggle or another.

The two southern nomes were the least civilized by the standards of Amun itself. Three Emperors of the past had extended the borders so far to the south that they had garnered in peoples of different races, beliefs, and customs —alien to the Old Knowledge, ever a source of trouble which smoldered into fire now and then. While the western nomes—they contained the trade cities where the barbarians brewed their own kind of poison for the disturbance of peace.

This was the trouble now. She arose and went once more to pacing. It was a fact, as she had assured Sela, that if Naldamak were truly dead she herself would know. The warning from kin to kin was a talent born in those of her family. But the mere fact that the Empress still lived was no assurance of her safety. She could well be in the hands of some secret force raised by Khasti. And what of the stranger who had come out of nowhere, even as Khasti had done, and had asked to see the Candace? What danger did he represent?

That Herihor was in command of the loyal forces in the north where the Candace might be expected to be found—that was the only faint point in their favor. That, and the fact that the talismen were still out of enemy hands. Anyway, she would have her chance to overhear what devil's brew Userkof or Idieze might be boiling here.

If Sela would only hurry! She did not want to miss any of the council hearing. Also—there was something she must not leave here. Tallahassee went to the chest and took out the bundle of the Rod and the Key. She would not feel safe anywhere away from them. There was no place in the chamber that would efficiently conceal the talismen if a strict search was made.

She had not forgotten that passage in the depths. Sela might think it well guarded by the alarm she mentioned, but an alarm would count for little against any attack by Khasti with the unknown forces he could control.

She dropped the bundle on the bed to tighten the fastenings about the roll of cloth. Yes, this she would take with her.

Tallahassee was still holding it, testing those fastenings when there was a click at the door and Sela sidled in, a number of towels clamped to her side by one of her bony elbows, both hands carrying a tall jar with care.

Look, Great Lady, is it not now even as you wished? Who would know the Princess Ashake in such a guise?"

Tallahassee stood once more before the mirror on the Candace's dressing table. Sela was very right. This was not Ashake whom she saw there. Her skin was again dark, even darker than it had been upon the first anointing which the Priestess had given her. Also, careful use of cosmetics had broadened her features, given a fullness that was not normal to her face.

She had folded about her head a sphinx linen cap, and the edges of that fell forward to further shadow and disguise her features. There was only her height which might betray her. But she did not plan to pace any well used corridor in open sight for long. And she could hope that no one would notice her, any more than any servant was noted when about her normal business.

The bundle she had made of the talismen was ready to

be carried in one of the wide baskets Sela had produced from an inner cupboard, intended for the transport of newly washed bed coverings.

But all this had taken time, very precious time. And the Council could well be in session. She stooped suddenly and set her painted lips to Sela's wrinkled cheek.

"Mother-in-fostering to my sister-kin," she said softly, "I give thanks to the Great Power that you have come to my aid. There is such service in this that not even the Blood could provide. On you be the blessing of That Which Holds Us All."

"Great Lady." Sela raised her hand and in turn touched a finger tip to Tallahassee's painted cheek. "Blessings and good fortune be on what you would do. If our dear Lady comes out of danger, what more can we ask? Wait you now, until I make certain that the corridor is empty. To be seen issuing from here . . ."

She was already on the way to the outer door when there was a scratching at it. Who? . . . Tallahassee hugged the basket tightly and her heart began to beat faster. Sela's head had cocked as she listened to that sound. Then, before Tallahassee could stop her, she swiftly opened the door.

It was Moniga who slipped through. But her neat uniform was gone. Like Tallahassee, the Amazon wore the dress of a servant, and she was breathing fast as she caught the door out of Sela's hold, shut it tight, and stood with her shoulders against it as if to form a barrier of her own body to hinder some pursuit.

"What is it?" Tallahassee demanded and saw the Amazon's look of surprise, her searching stare.

"Great Lady—but you? . . ." The girl was near to stammering.

"I go in another guise, yes. But what have you to tell us?"

"Great Lady, Assar went through the gate—and he

went readily. None saw him in the shadows. It was as if he knew, hound though he is, that he must not be sighted. But—when I returned—Great Lady, in the name of the Prince Userkof they had relieved the guard of the palace—"

Tallahassee heard Sela's hiss of breath.

"The Sworn Swords?"

"Great Lady—they were surrounded while I was gone on your order. They are now confined to the barracks. And the Captain—she was disarmed and taken away. They have laid upon the doors of the barracks that same barrier which is on the gates of the city. None can come forth."

"And it is men from the south who stand on guard?"

Moniga nodded. "Even so, Great Lady. I have seen the insignia of the Elephant on their uniforms. By now this palace is theirs. And I think that they are also changing the gate guards. These are barbarian warriors, Great Lady—some even wear the facial scars of the wild tribes."

"You have done very well," Tallahassee said slowly. "Now—stay you here with Sela, and be sure no one knows where you have taken refuge. There may come a time, maybe very soon, when I shall need a Sworn Sword at my back to be sure that no other's knife reaches me."

"Great Lady, what do you do? There are strangers in the Palace, more guards from the south—"

"That I know. But also I must learn more, for the sake of the Candace and perhaps of the Empire itself. Do not worry. This I do is something only I can accomplish, but it must be done."

For a moment, it seemed that Moniga would not stand back from the door. But as Tallahassee eyed her steadily the Amazon gave way.

"Great Lady," she made her plea, "take me with you! I have this." She reached hand into the bosom of her dress and brought out a hand weapon.

"That we may have need for later. No—this way, I go alone. It is a secret of the Candace that only I also may know—and it will be to our aid. Sela, keep closed this door—do not even open should the maid you mentioned come to it. Khasti has weapons past our knowledge, and some of them are our own people constrained to his will. It was the use of such that brought me into his hands. Do not open this door!"

"The will has spoken, so be it." Sela gave formal answer. Moniga looked as if she would protest once again, but Tallahassee slipped quickly through, and the nurse shut it firmly behind her.

Luckily she did not have far to go. Those who had planned this secret, upon the building of the "new" palace some three hundred years ago, had wished it to be quickly accessible to the ruler. She stood for a moment, listening intently.

There was a series of arched openings to her left, giving to the Candace's private courtyard garden. Through those poured sunlight, and it was the strong western sun of afternoon. She could hear the sounds of birds, the scream of one of those peacocks bred from gifts of an Indian ruler two or three generations ago. It was a shattering sound, enough at this moment to make her start.

But the corridor itself was empty. Since the Candace was known to be gone, there were no guards along it. Tallahassee sped swiftly along, hugging the right wall, as far from the arches as she could get.

The garden corridor gave upon a room the rulers had used in the past for more private audiences. There was a smaller, less impressive throne chair, some stools-of-honor for visiting members of the Blood, but for the most part it was bare.

However, beyond the door that led out of it, Tallahassee could hear a murmur of voices. Yes, the council was gathering! She must be very swift and quiet.

She rounded the wall of the lesser audience chamber to the southern corner where there were panels of carved wood, oiled and polished with preservative. Placing the basket at her feet, she raised her hands to fit them into the spaces she had been drilled to find so many years ago. She had not forgotten, or rather Ashake had not. Her fingers went easily into depressions one could not perceive because of the depth and high relief of the carving. Now she swung almost her full weight downward.

There was a scrape of sound, which made her glance hastily around. Then the stubborn controls, unused probably for years, worked. Two of the panels opened and she crawled through then stooped to drag the basket after her before she shut that cramped door.

It was not dark—light beamed from one side, and it was there that she crouched to watch and listen—being well able to see all that was beyond through a fretwork of carving so intricate that it concealed well its purpose on the other side of the wall.

The Council Chamber might be new to Tallahassee, but Ashake memory found it familiar, though she recognized only two of the six men sitting there—General Itua of the Southern Army, and the Nomarch of the Elephant Nome. There was no sign of Khasti, whom she thought surely would be present, nor was either Userkof nor Idieze here.

However, she had no more seated herself in the restricted crouch her present quarters permitted than the door opened and Idieze swept in, with a fan bearer in her wake.

She dared! Ashake memory gave fuel to anger—that one dares to usurp honors Naldamak never would grant her! She must be very sure that both the Candace and Ashake herself were removed or immobilized. Had Khasti not informed her then that his prisoner had escaped?

Khasti believed this woman and her husband were

tools to be used and discarded. Idieze herself had come to Ashake to strike a bargain, or pretend to. What then had changed so that now the Princess believed she could call a council and be obeyed?

"This is a time of grave matters," Idieze spoke abruptly, cutting through the murmurs of formal greeting, waving the men back to their seats. "You have been summoned, my Lords, at the call of my husband, the Prince Userkof, who, though he lies stricken with a fever, still knows that the safety of the Empire is above all else, the matter depending upon the strength of such as you—who have been loyal to him."

She paused as she looked swiftly from one face to another, catching the eyes of each in turn and holding that straight stare for a breath or two, as if she so issued some warning or demanded in return another protestation of loyalty. Perhaps she was satisfied by what she saw for now she continued:

"It is now well known that the Candace is lost in the desert storm. And that anyone whose flyer's caught in such fury could survive is not to be believed. And the Princess Ashake—she has of her own will turned aside from the rule, taking instead the final oath of the Temple, tying herself to that service for the rest of her life."

So? Now that was clever, Ashake acknowledged. Her long absences from New Napata on Temple business had left few here who knew her personally. And those who would be her firmest champions to bring her to the throne—Zyhlarz, Jayta, and Herihor—were most conveniently removed from this council. These men would accept the fact that she might do this, mainly because they wished to believe so.

"The Heir must make such statements before the Council, and then at the High Altar before all the representatives of the Guilds and the Masters, as well as the Nomarchs." The man who wore the badge of the Leopard spoke. He used none of the customary honorifics in addressing Idieze.

Ashake did not know him except by name, which was Takarka, for he had only recently come to the heirship of that westernmost land of the Empire, and that upon the death of a distant cousin. But he had dealt much with the white-skinned barbarians of the north and she had automatically judged him to be of the kind that could be suborned by Khasti. To have such a statement out of him was a surprise now.

"Which she shall do at the proper time. Though nothing can be done yet," Idieze covered smoothly, "until the certain death of our Son-in-Glory be certified as the truth. In the meantime, the Heir has withdrawn to a place of distant meditation and the Empire cannot rule itself."

"Surely, surely," muttered General Itua to second that.

"If the Heir has not yet sworn openly," persisted Takarka, "then she must be summoned. . . ."

It was he who now looked from face to face at his companions as if surprised that no voice had been raised to back him.

"It is the Law," he spoke shortly and sharply.

"In times of crisis"—the Nomarch of the Elephant answered that—"law cannot always be relied upon. The tribes beyond the wardship of my own land grow restless. A firm hand is needed to keep them in check. Let them learn that we have no ruler and they will accept that as a sign to invade. It took us two full years to best them before, and that was a hundred years ago. There is good reason to believe that they have been trading with the northern barbarians. There are rumors and more than rumors of their getting weapons to match or even outmatch what we can put in the field against them."

General Itua grunted. "Do not give heed to this constant downcrying of our fitness," he snapped. "Perhaps we also have something now that will surprise them—and others. What, Lady"—he looked directly at Idieze—"of the forces of the north? What part will they play—for or against your Royal Husband? It is said that there is an old grievance between him and the Prince General. And the Prince General is not only of the Blood, but his betrothal to the Heir still stands. Think you that he will step tamely aside if there is such a division in this land?"

Idieze's mouth tightened. "Just as you warn that our army may have secrets not open to public knowledge, General, so do I say that there are other secrets. If Prince Herihor seeks the throne against all custom, he will never even enter the gates of New Napata—alive!"

The Nomarch of the Leopard leaned forward a little on his stool-of-the-presence.

"I have heard that there is a stranger in Napata—one with new knowledge. Is he the secret of whom you speak, Lady? If so—why is he not here to let us see and hear him? We have kept our land because we have not thrown aside that which was our greatest gift, in Khem and afterwards. The barbarians depend upon what they make with their two hands—and look at the history of their lands. Have they aught to boast of? The death of kings, some struck down by jealous rivals upon their own seats-of-honor, the killing of men with only short seasons of uneasy peace in which they can prepare once more for the flood of blood across their countries. I have heard them boast of this—deeming it honorable—for honor is for the victor, not the crushed. I have heard them convict themselves with their own boasting.

"How many wars have we of Amun fought?" He held out one hand, fingers spread, and touched the fingertip of the other hand to each he named.

"In the far past we expelled the Hyksos who had taken Khem, later we fought with those from the north—three times. We broke finally because we were few and they were many, pouring in new hordes where, when one of our Blood fell, there were none to rise up in his place. Before them we were driven south—to Meroë.

"But our other weapon grew the stronger. Men could fight with mind and spirit—not to conquer the aggressors but to send them back, into their own place. Meroë we held against the men from the east until our faith thinned and we were bereft of our strongest shield. So again we traveled, this time west. And there, under Rameses the Lion, we built this New Napata, and we were not moved again!

"Rather did our fires burn brighter and we learned and grew—so Amun was born. Five wars in all—and one rebellion from the south in near eight thousand years. No northern cluster of barbarian states can match that."

"My Lord." Idieze spoke earnestly. "All you say is the truth. But this is also true—we have come again to a time when the Talent runs thin, fewer are born with the seeds of the Power in them. Even the line of the Blood has dwindled, is that not so? This is becoming again such a time as you cite, in the past, when we weaken in that which has defended us. Therefore, that Amun may continue to exist, we shall be driven, in our great need, to other weapons. This is not what we want but it is a fact we must face.

"And one of our greatest defenses is a secure throne. If we have not that, how then can we marshal the nation?"

Clever, clever, clever—Ashake wanted to spit like a battle-inflamed cat. Idieze's logic was unanswerable.

"Can Userkof hold the Power then?" For the first time the Nomarch of the River Horse spoke. He was a man of middle years and, Ashake had heard it said, of more than a little cunning, preferring to get his way by intrigue rather than open action. His obese form must find it uncomfortable, perching on the small stool, and his eyes were always near half-closed as if he were stupid—but he was not.

"He is of the Blood!" Idieze returned sharply.

"And the Power itself?"

"Is safe!" she answered, perhaps too quickly. The Nomarch of the River Horse was the last man Ashake would want to lie to without a wealth of seeming conviction behind her falsehood. But perhaps Idieze, moved by the shortness of time, could do nothing else. What if they demanded that the Rod and the Key be produced here and now?

"Where is Zyhlarz?" It was Takarka again. "And the Nomarchs of the north? This is not a full council, and so we can put forth no decisions."

"The north—" Idieze hesitated. "My lords, this is a grievous thing I must tell you—the northern army has proved traitor. They have declared for Herihor. And think you—who has searched for our Sun-in-Glory— who?"

She made of that question an accusation.

"You have proof?" Takarka faced her.

"Why think you Zyhlarz is not here? The Temple is sealed for mourning. But we cannot prove what we have heard. Only, would the Prince General dare to put on the Lion Helm unless our Lady is safely dead? If he has found her—he has said nothing, thinking to use the time to argue with the Heir, and so rule in her name as her Royal Husband—"

"We can make no decisions without a full council," Takarka said firmly. "Let Userkof stand before us with the Power, and we shall know the truth: that the Candace is indeed dead and the Heir has put aside her claim. For only he who is the rightful ruler may so appear."

"That is well said, my Lord," the Nomarch of the River Horse agreed.

He of the Elephant was hesitant for only a space and then nodded, also. General Itua's eyes were on the floor before him, as if his mind roved elsewhere, and he did not speak at all, while the other Nomarch, a nervous little man with a twitching eyelid, was quick to nod.

Idieze arose. Her face was a smooth mask, but Ashake could feel her seething anger—and beneath that anger was fear. Had this move been made without the knowledge of Khasti, a desperate attempt to get the support of those nobles she believed would back her even against the reputed resources of the stranger? Ashake began to think so as the Princess swept out of the room, sparing no word of farewell to any of those summoned.

"Userkof." The Nomarch of the Elephant had said only that one word when his fellow southerner opened his eyes wide for the first time and stared for an instant at him.

"Not here—not now, yes," the General said cryptically as he got to his feet awkwardly, nearly as if he had been as heavy and shapeless of body as the man on his left.

They did not leave together, the southerners going first, then the General nearly on their heels, still looking preoccupied, as if he must at once make sure that the troops under him *did* have the weapons of which he had spoken. The two remaining Nomarchs did not draw together— rather he of the Leopard pushed past the other, and the last man looked after him, wearing an expression Ashake could not read.

She was hot of body in this cubby and hotter yet of mind with frustration. There was no possible way she could spy on them outside this room. They would be housed in the Wing of Noble Visitors with their own guards very much in evidence, since their masters were plainly unsettled in their own minds. There she could not play the part even of a palace maid without fear of being uncovered.

And she had learned so little. Much of that might be guessing. There seemed to be one holdout in the ranks of the enemy—the Nomarch of the Leopard. But she could not order that he be trusted merely on what she had overheard here. However, it was a little comforting to believe that there *were* doubters and that the councillors were not ready to back Idieze in some sudden action. The more time they were given. . . .

They? Of what did the Royal forces within New Napata now consist? A woman so old she had seen two generations, a single Amazon in disguise, armed with nothing but her hand-weapon, a maid on whom they might or might not be able to depend—and herself, whether she wanted that so or not. In this she was caught and forced to fight Ashake's battle, if not for the sake of Amun, for her own life.

She made the trip back to the Candace's suite, noting that the sun had lost much of its hold on the gallery floor since she had come. The burning sun of the desert—how long could Naldamak survive if it were true her flyer had been lost in a storm. Even if she had lived through its crash, the harsh conditions of that land gave no promise of more than a day or two of further existence.

Yet, she was not dead. For Ashake would have known. Of that somehow Tallahassee was convinced. She had reached the door of the outer chamber and now she scratched her signal on its surface, glancing right and left hurriedly as she did so, the basket containing the talismen balanced precariously on her hip.

They must have been waiting right by the door, for it was speedily flung open. And the Amazon was so moved by her concern, that, thinking nothing of rank, she put out a calloused, hard-fingered hand to draw Tallahassee in as quickly as she could.

"They could not agree," the girl told the two who awaited her. "The Nomarch of the Leopard leads the opposition to Idieze's demands. But she has told them two tales—that the Candace is dead, or possibly prisoner to Herihor—and that he leads a rebellion against the throne!"

"Lies!" Sela hissed.

"So we know. But proof is another thing. Khasti was not there—perhaps she called this council without his knowledge. I believe she fears him—and rightly. If we could only build upon these divisions within their own ranks! If I had but the backing of the Son-of-Apedemek, and even two or three from the Temple, it might be possible to work upon their jealousies and fears—"

"Great Lady!" Sela had come to her side as she stood, the bundle of the Rod and Key in her hands, frustration bitter in her. "You hold," the nurse reminded her, "that which is the heart and soul of Amun—can you not draw upon its Power?"

Tallahassee started. If she were truly Ashake—yes. But those gaps in the Ashake memory were so large. She could summon the two to her as she had in that laboratory, but other uses for them—those were part of the knowledge that had *not* been imparted by the tapes. But—she might try—the Temple! That could be closed to physical entrance, but was it also shut to the power of thought? If she could contact Zyhlarz, in whose mind lay the deepest layers of the Wisdom in this generation! . . .

She turned upon the other two.

"There is something I may try. You must guard me well, for it may be that what is truly me must quest beyond the realms of the flesh that holds me."

"Be sure, Great Lady," the Amazon answered first, "that we shall do what we can. Though where—?"

"With any fortune perhaps to Zyhlarz." If they knew the truth, they might be more zealous. "Now let me prepare."

SHE floated in space which did not exist in any world she knew. Before her was a tall, dark wall, holding her back from what she sought. Zyhlarz, the others of the Upper Way, were behind that. But this path was closed—at least to one who had not all of what Ashake had once known.

Baffled, Tallahassee tried again and again to pierce that wall, haunted by the thought that the fault lay in herself, in the imperfect memory she had been given. She lacked the deepest secrets of their schooling. And whether this wall was of the enemy's devising, or born of the need for defense against some psychic attack, that she did not know either.

Though Khasti might not have raised such a barrier in this between-the-worlds place, there were those from the far south (the medicine men of the wild tribes) who held perverted and dark powers—who would fear above

all else the Light of the Temple. And they might well
have been harnessed by the rebel forces.

The wall held; she was wearied and defeated by it. In
this place her half-knowledge could not hold her safely
for too long. Yet she still clung to a fragment of hope.

Then . . .

Before the wall there flashed a column of pure flame
as golden as the mask Jayta wore. Out of that flame arose
that mask itself to face the disembodied Ashake.

Daughter-of-Apedemek?—There was no speech in this
place which could be shaped by lips and tongue, for only
a sense of identity existed.

I come. The mask image answered her.

There is great need . . .

There is greater that you win to us, Sister-in-the-
Light . . .

How may I do this? demanded the Ashake-self.

Seek once more the lower ways. There are secrets
there that can lead you. You have done very well, and
fortune has favored you. There will be those—

But a cry rent the air and at that sound the shadow
world fragmented and was gone. Ashake-Tallahassee—
was whipped by a force greater than any wind, driven
away from the wall, from the light that was Jayta. She
could not escape that overwhelming pressure. Then came
a sense of anchorage, or return. The girl opened her eyes
dazedly.

Two lamps threw queer shadows on the ceiling above.
And nearby she heard a faint moaning. Somehow, in
spite of the vast weariness that burdened her, she managed to turn her head.

Someone crouched there, hands across her face. And,
as Tallahassee groggily pulled herself up, she saw that
another body lay upon the floor. That small crumpled
form—Sela! And that other, shaking with terror—the

Amazon Moniga. But what had struck here? Some attack launched by Khasti?

She put feet to the floor, sat up, though she wavered in her slow movements.

"Be still!" Her voice was low, but she put into it all the sharp authority she could now summon.

The Amazon did not raise her head, her moans were growing louder. Somehow Tallahassee stood up and took two steps to the side of the women. She leaned over, in spite of the peril to her own balance, and struck Moniga across the cheek. For the Amazon had lifted her head to show a face near witless with what could only be sheer terror. And knowing of the Spartan training that had shaped her, Tallahassee could readily believe that whatever had sent her into this state must have been well beyond any normal experience.

"Be still!" she said fiercely. Then those staring eyes focused upon her and a little of the blank panic faded from the other's face.

Tallahassee fell to her knees, her hands going out to the still form of Sela. At first she thought that the old woman was dead, then her searching fingers found the faintest of pulse beats.

"Help me!" She gave a second order.

The Amazon moved stiffly, as one who answered orders without understanding them. Together they managed to get Sela up on the bed Tallahassee had just quitted. Her small, wizened face was very pale, almost greenish, and her mouth opened slackly, a thin thread of moisture running from one corner.

"Wine," Tallahassee ordered. "Bring wine." Under her hands Sela's body felt very cold. The old woman was in shock. The girl drew up the covers about her; and when Moniga, her hands still shaking so that the wine nearly spilled, brought her a goblet, Tallahassee raised the nurse's head to her own shoulder, supporting her so that she might dribble into that mouth a little of the liquid.

Sela choked, gasped, and swallowed. Her pulse was growing stronger. Tallahassee settled her back on the bed, turned to the Amazon.

"Tell me, Moniga, what happened?"

Luckily the girl appeared to have recovered something of both her courage and her wits. Now when Tallahassee looked at her she flushed as if ashamed.

"Great Lady—it—there were *things* . . ." she half stuttered. "I fought with the Sworn Swords at Menkani when the desert men broke into the Fort and we went to retake it. I have seen much, Great Lady, that was full of horror. But this—this was not of our world!"

"In what way?" Tallahassee asked quietly, knowing that she must use patience.

"When you were asleep, they came. They were like shadows—or a kind of troubling in the air. How can I find the words to describe what I have never seen before? But they were—they were angry in some manner and their hate—it could be felt!"

The wraiths again.

"I myself have seen these things, Moniga. They do exist. And I believe I know what they may be seeking. Only I have not the power to give it to them."

"Great Lady—they gathered about you as you lay. And when we tried to protect you—they . . ." Moniga's hands went to her head. "Somehow they got into our minds—with terrible thoughts. They would have me kill . . . But I held out against that, Great Lady—I did!

"Then they brought pain and the Lady Sela cried out. I thought she was dead. And when they turned on me— Great Lady, I was not sure how long I could hold against them! I think I screamed—"

"You could do no else, Sworn Sword. These things are not to be met by any weapon one can hold in hand.

That you resisted their strength is a battle of honor for you," Tallahassee reassured her.

She had gained at least a part of Jayta's message. But to seek again the lower passages, where the wraiths had hung before, when she did not believe that this time she could expect anything but hostility from them, was perilous indeed. She sat on the edge of the bed and tried to think. Sela seemed to be sleeping naturally. Her face had lost the stamp of intolerable fear. And Moniga was herself again.

"Listen well now." Tallahassee knew that there was no escape for her. Jayta's message had been very clear. She would have to win free from New Napata, and there was only one way, that which led through those slimed passages below. "There are things I need—for I have received a message from the Daughter-of-Apedemek through the way of the Talent. Can you find and bring these to me in secret?

"Great Lady, it is ordered, so it is done," Moniga replied with the formal salute of her rank.

"These then—provisions—such as the army takes for maneuvers—enough in a shoulder sack for several days. Also a night torch with a newly fitted unit. Bring these as speedily as possible. And with them bread, meat, what I may eat at once."

"These I can get, Great Lady." Moniga was already moving to the door.

When that had closed behind the Amazon, Tallahassee set to work. Her strength had returned a little, and she must not allow herself to imagine ahead, as to what it might be like to be caught somewhere in that thick darkness below by the wraiths. No, think rather of what she must do right now.

She went through the chest of Naldamak's clothing to find what she needed—the uniform the Empress wore when reviewing her troops on formal occasions. Using scissors from the dressing table, she cut away all the insignia of rank, leaving a one-piece garment, not unlike what her own world called a jump suit.

It was a little tight for her across the chest, but she was able to fasten the buckles, and luckily the boots fitted, though they cramped her feet after the looseness of the sandals. Sela still slept—dreamlessly, Tallahassee hoped.

The talismen she would have to carry bare. But, lest she might drop them, she looped cords about each to fasten around her wrist. She covered her head with a scarf knotted under her chin. She was finishing that when she heard the signal and let Moniga in.

A sack, well-filled, hung from the Amazon's shoulder, and she balanced a tray on which was the food Tallahassee had asked for. As the girl sat to eat and drink she gave her last orders.

"I leave here, Sworn Sword, by a hidden way. Do you hold guard and see that the Lady Sela wants for no attention. Keep secret that I have been here if you are discovered. And watch well the way I go so that none can come upon you secretly."

"Great Lady, I would go with you." Moniga had changed into her uniform and her weapon swung at her belt.

"Not so. This is a path where only the Rod can lead me. You will offer greater service by guarding this door. It may be that when I return I shall come again by this way, perhaps bringing help with me. We must be sure, should that be our plan, that we do not walk into an ambush."

"Great Lady—be sure that I shall keep such guard!"

Tallahassee shouldered the bag of provisions. She looped the cords of Key and Rod about her left wrist, picked up the torch with the other. At her order Moniga held aside the wall hanging and she entered the secret way. There was a jingle and she remembered Sela's setting an alarm. To the Amazon she explained that signal before she set off down into the dark.

This time the hand torch gave her far more light than the radiance by which she had earlier come, its ray cutting clearly to light step and wall. And it was not long before she reached the ancient walled door and crawled through the break into that place of bad smells and suggestion of lurking danger.

Orientating herself by the palace above, Tallahassee turned left into the unknown way. The stair was one of those secrets of another age, probably constructed first as an escape for the Royal Family should disaster strike as it had at Meroë. Therefore, there must be some exit outside the city. And that, she hoped, would not be guarded by the barriers Khasti had set.

The moisture and fetid smells were both stronger. She had to pick a careful path as the footing was slimy enough so now and then her boots slipped. The beam of her torch caught for an instant the raised head of a creature—either a large lizard or a snake. But it flicked out of sight as if light were a threat. She had expected an assault from the wraiths (after all this might well be their lurking place) and was constantly waiting for it, not daring to allow herself to relax even when time passed and that did not develop.

Moisture gathered here in viscid, evil-smelling pools which she skirted as best she could. Then the corridor ended in a sullen flood from which arose such a stench as she did not believe could be breathed for long. She tucked her torch for the moment into her belt and drew down the kerchief that covered her head to enfold her mouth and nose in a vain attempt to filter out some of the nastiness.

The flood was fast flowing, and she was sure this was one of the main sewers of the city. How deep that offal-filled stream was she had no idea. She hesitated. The way stopped here. Which meant that whoever followed it had to take to the sewer at this point. But to venture out into that with no idea of depth, when she could be swept from her feet and rolled under the filth to drown? No, she must find some other way.

Bracing one shoulder against the wall, Tallahassee leaned forward as far as she dared, to flash the beam of the torch along the wall toward her right, for the passage had met with the sewer at a sharp angle. There did exist a footpath—if one could call it that, for it was hardly wider than her two feet put side to side. Though the flood lapped only a little below its edge, yet it was thickly encrusted with foul deposits that higher waves must have left.

To take that way was to risk her footing at every step, yet there was no alternative. And how long could she breathe this polluted air without succumbing? There was no use in lingering—if this was the road, then it was the one she must take.

She squeezed around the corner where passage and sewer met to step gingerly out on that befouled ledge. Her guess had been very right. Here the slime of the inner corridor became a thicker morass that sucked at her feet every time she raised one for another step. She had to move so slowly that the foul air grew more and more of a threat to consciousness.

Tallahassee lost all track of time. Her head ached, and she felt nauseated, dizzy. Once a scaled head arose from the flood and jaws opened, to close with a snap when she flashed the light directly into small, vicious eyes. A crocodile—luckily not large enough to be a true menace, and it seemed to hate the light. But where there was one there might well be more.

She came suddenly to a niche in the wall that contained a sealed door and flashed her light within. There had been an arch farther back, but like the one she had broken through in the other passage, this also had been filled in. She edged herself within this larger space and tried to think more clearly.

If her calculations were correct, this sealed door was in the wrong direction to go beyond the walls. And in her present state she was not sure she could even use the power of the Rod enough to tumble a single of the locking stones. Better to go on—the sewer *did* have a place to emerge, that she could be sure of.

She longed to rest in the small place she had found, save that the air here was no better than in the sewer channel. So, reluctantly, she groped her way on. She couldn't be sure, but hadn't the height of the water pouring along beside her begun to drop? The ledge was level and had not climbed. Also—almost she could believe that now the air was less foul. She braced herself again and flashed the torch overhead. There the light caught on the edge of a well-like opening which she was seeing from the reverse, from its bottom. Also, there showed a series of hoops large enough to hold with a hand, rest a boot upon, extending upwards into the well. Outside the wall of the city, or in? She was afraid this still was in. There would be no reason to set such an opening without the walls. And if she were to expend her strength to climb it, and then find she was still a prisoner . . . She did not believe that she would be able then to make herself descend again into this place of stench.

Yet an unknown opening *within* the city. Something stirred far back in her mind; she could not yet clarify it.

Step by uncertain step she moved on along the ledge. Now there was no mistaking that the water *had* dropped. So, the stone she trod was less befouled, patches of the rock from which it had been hewn showed clear here and there. Also, the air cleared somewhat.

She—

At that moment they struck; when she had been lulled into forgetting them. The wraiths made their attack upon her mind not her body. She staggered, but she did not fall. Nor did she drop the torch. Rather she put her shoulders to the wall, as if she could so protect her back, and swung her light back and forth across the water.

There was movement there. Not of the wraiths but perhaps of some creature they summoned to pull her down.

"If I die here," she said between set teeth to the empty air—empty to her sight, yet alive with a company she could sense—"then do your hopes fail. I have not in me the power to help you. But there are others greater and stronger than I, and those I seek. Do you wish in me now the death of your chance, as well as that of my body?"

The thing in the water was coming closer. Still she could detect no waver in the air.

"Akini." She called the only name she knew. "I have told you the full truth!"

Still they hung there in menace, and she could not distinguish among them that one stronger identity to which she had given name. There was a swirl of water as a hideous, armored head broke the surface of the sewer, its jaws agape enough to show stained teeth. This crocodile was not the small one she had earlier sighted. It must be old, so long a swimmer in this place of rottenness that it carried in it all the evil years could accumulate.

Tallahassee grasped the Rod tightly. Against this thing out of the foulness of ages she had only that. As she had raised the Rod by her will to lift the protective cage Khasti had set over it, so now did she swing its point toward the thing that was hitching its scaled body higher. Massive, clawed forepaws reached for the ledge on which she stood.

Power—

The light she trained on that cruel head had no effect. It had been urged to attack by the influences of those who now watched avidly from out of the darkness.

Power!

Tallahassee schooled herself not to scream. The sewer dweller embodied all that was of nightmare.

Power, she demanded of Ashake memory—give me that which you know and have used. Give me—or I—we die!

From the point of the Rod there shot a line of fire more fiercely brilliant by far than the torch. It struck between the small eyes of the crocodile. The creature gave a bellow which echoed so harshly through the narrow tunnel, the sound continued to ring in her ears even as, kicking, it fell back and the flood covered it once more. The girl watched it disappear, hardly believing that Ashake memory had so answered her.

Did that memory have an identity? It could not, it was a thing that had been taped, forced into her own mind by the technology of these people. Ashake was dead. Yet more and more did Ashake sustain her—could a memory mold another?

They were still there—the wraiths. But they would not try that again. There was a hesitancy about them that she could sense. They were drawn by what she carried, but there was a fear underlying their need.

She waited for a long moment for some further attack, some blow from the unseen. When that did not come she spoke again.

"I have made a bargain with you, Akini. But I cannot fulfill it unless you give me a chance to draw together those who know where you are and what holds you. I do not forget—nor shall I."

They were there still, but no answer came. She could

wait no longer. Resolutely Tallahassee started on, but she knew the wraiths followed after. Let them—if they wished.

There came a curve in the water tunnel. And a breath of clean air puffed into her face. Somewhere, not too far ahead, must lie the exit from this waterway. She switched off the torch, standing still for a moment or two until her eyes adjusted and she could see by the radiance of the Rod and Key. Then step by very cautious step she advanced.

There was an opening, one crossed by bars. Through a lower exit spilt the wash of the sewer, but this was higher, near the ledge. She hurried toward it for the path here was relatively free of slime. Then she jerked off the covering about her nose and mouth, sucking avidly at the sweet air.

She thrust the torch inside her uniform for safekeeping and began to trace the bars of the grill with her hands. Outside it was night, and there seemed to be a stiff wind blowing. Grit and dust sifted through the grill, making her cough.

Though she found where the bars were embedded in a frame, she had not yet discovered any fastening on this side. And it was secure, yielding not an inch under her pull. The Rod—must she cut her way through—

From the outside came a sound, freezing her hands on the metal grill, making her alert and tense. There was a soft whine—a shadow pushed against the bars.

She smelled the scent of dog.

Assar? Had the hound just gone beyond the gates and then roamed around the city? Her hope had been so slender that she did not realize how much she had built on it until this moment.

"Assar?" She whispered the name.

There was an excited bark and she realized her folly. That sound was enough to alert any human ears in the vicinity. And it could well be that Khasti or the southern Nomarchs had their men outside the locked wall.

"Ashake?"

A whisper in return—one she had not expected to hear. "Who? . . ."

"Ashake—Jayta had said you would come—in this way. You are here?"

"Herihor?" She had almost called "Jason."

"Yes, my lady. And you shall be out speedily—stand back a little."

She withdrew along the ledge a pace or two. There was another shadow before the grill, and she heard the grate of metal against metal. Then something gave—the grate fell outward, and she heard a grunt as if Herihor had not expected it to be so easy.

Seconds later she heard him call.

"Come, Lady, the way is open."

He was reaching forward to draw her into the clean air of the night.

THE group in the tent was mixed. In this war council they held nearly equal rank. Jayta sat next to Tallahassee, and beyond her was Herihor, to the right, the Candace Naldamak. To her left were two northern generals and the Colonel of the Sworn Swords.

Tallahassee's mouth and throat felt dry. She had been talking steadily ever since Herihor had brought her here, going over the details of the laboratory where Khasti wrought his mysteries, the passage she had found. On a piece of paper Herihor himself had sketched out the underground ways as she remembered them. And by Naldamak's hand lay the Key and the Rod.

The Candace was spare and thin, her face, fine-boned under the dark skin, was older than Ashake memory had painted it for Tallahassee. But there was no mistaking the quick light of intelligence in her dark eyes, the way she caught pertinent facts in Tallahassee's recital and asked for a report in detail.

"Khasti!" the Candace said as Tallahassee finished.

"Always Khasti." She turned her head to speak to the general on her left.

"Nastasen, what have your scouts discovered in the desert lands?"

"Sun-in-Glory, the report of the desert rovers is that years ago this stranger was found by a dead camel and brought by them to one of our patrols, since he superficially resembles a man of Amun. They believed then that he was an outlaw fleeing our justice. But there is another story, newer, that a second man has recently come out of the same quarter of desert and this one is like unto Khasti. However, he asked not for his fellow, but rather for your Glory. And he was sent on to New Napata to await your pleasure—even as the Heir has reported his coming. This man's camel bags were searched, in secret, and found to contain a very small amount of rations as if he had come from only a short distance.

"Therefore, after he passed, the Captain of a Hundred at that fort sent out another patrol to trace him. They came to a valley among the rocks and, though no wall could be seen there, yet there was a barrier through which no man could force his way."

"And this was the man who came to New Napata?"

"He was seen to walk from out the gates, those sealed gates, Glory, and then he disappeared."

"So what is a barrier to us is not to these strangers," cut in Herihor.

But the Candace spoke again: "As you know, I and my people were found by a desert patrol. But we would not have lived had not two strangers come out of nowhere earlier, given us food and water, and pointed us the direction to follow. I am beginning to think that Khasti may have his enemies among his own kind, whatever or wherever they may be. But the core of his strength lies in New Napata and there he must be faced. Sister"—

she smiled at Tallahassee—"very well have you wrought within the city, and outside it, too. We owe you the return of these," she gestured toward the talismen, "and now a chance to attack Khasti in his own lair. Userkof and his play at treason—that does not matter at the moment. It is this stranger who furnishes such rebels with their strength.

"You have marshalled your advance force." She looked to Herihor. "Can they be fed through this noxious tunnel, so to strike not only in the palace, but in the city, and, most of all, at the nest of Khasti?"

"Glory, give but the command," he replied swiftly. "If they know you live, most of the city will rise at your war cry."

"Then let it be done!" ordered the Candace. "Only strike not at the nest, merely guard it until we come." She nodded to Jayta and Tallahassee. "For with the Temple immobilized, we three may be the only ones with the Greater Knowledge to be used against whatever devilishness this Khasti devises—"

Jayta suddenly raised her head, not to look to Naldamak but back over her shoulder. Their conference tent was well guarded. Sworn Swords and picked men of Herihor's own guard formed its defense. And they had spoken in low voices that could not be overheard. But now the priestess's hand swept up in a commanding gesture which silenced even the Candace, who watched her with narrowed eyes.

"There is one coming." Jayta's voice was hardly above a whisper. "A stranger—"

Naldamak made a small sign and the priestess arose from her stool, looped back a fraction of the hanging door curtain, and peered out. A moment later she nodded to the Candace.

"It is not Khasti. But one of his breed."

Herihor's expression was that of rising anger. "How

did such come through the outer guard?" he demanded fiercely, perhaps not of them but of those guards.

"It appears," Naldamak said thoughtfully, "that such as he can do this. For those who came to us in the desert we did not see before they stood there before us. Bring him to me."

"Glory—" One of the generals began a protest. But Naldamak shook her head at him.

"If I owe my life and those of my people to such a man, I do not believe he intends to harm me now. Bring him in, Daughter-of-Apedemek!"

The priestess bowed her head in assent and slipped out of the door. But Herihor and the two generals ostentatiously drew their hand weapons and kept them at ready. Tallahassee moved a little on her folding stool so that she could better see whoever entered.

For a second or two as he stooped his head to come under the hanging Jayta pulled aside for him, for he was a tall man, she was sure that by some trick Khasti himself had won into the heart of their camp. And she half arose to call out a warning. Then she saw that even if they were of the same race there was a difference between the newcomer and him who held New Napata to his will.

This one wore the robes of a desert raider, yet she could sense they were not his natural dress. And he was older, though he had an air of inborn authority such as one of the Blood might show. As he faced Naldamak he raised one hand, palm out, in a salute they did not understand but realized was one of dignity meeting dignity, of peer facing peer.

"You are the Candace Naldamak." That was half-question, half-statement.

"That is the truth." Herihor leaned forward a little, his suspicion plain to read on his open face. "And who are you, outlander?"

"It does not matter who I am," the man replied with the same authority as was in his manner of walking, of being. "Your Empress owes her life to us. Now we ask something in return."

"I know you . . ." Naldamak said slowly. "You were the third man in the desert, the one who stood aside and did not approach us. Yes, I owe you life and the lives of those who are my most faithful servants. What do you want of us in return?"

"There is one in the city, of our own blood and kind. He has offended against our custom and laws by coming here. Even as we offend in seeking him. But this we must do, no matter what price we will pay later. He has taken your city, he wishes to rule here. Do not count him as an unimportant enemy, Candace Naldamak, for when he fled from whence we all come, he brought with him devices beyond the comprehension of your world. Those must be destroyed, the man taken. But we are bound by oath not to loose upon him our own weapons. . . ."

Jayta had returned quietly to the group, but she did not reseat herself. Instead she stood staring at the stranger. Tallahassee caught puzzlement and then a dawning wonder which was half awe in her expression. Suddenly the priestess's hand rose in the air and with a finger she traced some pattern strange even to Ashake memory.

The man fronting Naldamak turned his head, met Jayta's stare, to return that with something near to menace in his look.

"What do you?" he demanded.

Deliberately, for the second time, Jayta traced that symbol.

"You can't know—" For the first time his outer self-confidence cracked somewhat, and then quickly he added:

"That such knowledge remains—"

"After all these centuries?" Jayta completed his sentence. "I am the Daughter-of-Apedemek, in the direct spiritual line, oh, far traveler, from those who—"

"No!" His gesture was forbidding. "That you know at all is contrary to all we believed. But if you do, then you also recognize what this Khasti is and that he has no place here. It is a great and final sin that he has come."

Naldamak looked from the stranger to Jayta and then back again. Then she spoke decisively.

"We do not gather here to argue about what part of this world Khasti came from, but how we may handle him. You say, man out of the desert, that he has devices beyond our control. Yet you will not yourself go up against him. How then do you think we may handle him?" And she made of that question a challenge.

"Only get him out of his own place, or the place he has made his own, and he will be ours to take."

Herihor laughed without mirth. "A small deed and one easily accomplished, would you say? Why not net your own fish, stranger? We have learned there are inner ways to his hole, and we shall be only too ready to show them to you."

"I can take no part in your battles, Prince General. Even as your own priests, I have certain restraints laid upon me which I cannot break. But this I warn you—if you come by secret into this place of his, destroy it utterly. There are devices there which, used by the unwary, could not only turn New Napata into dust to pollute the earth, but would also loose death on all your world. He came well prepared for what he would do."

"Retake perhaps an ancient heritage?" Tallahassee did not know where those words came from, or why she said them aloud. It was as if she repeated something that was born of neither of the memories that were hers.

Now that searching, near menacing stare was turned on her. She felt an odd sensation, a probing at her thoughts. Instinctively she tightened the guard that Ashake knew, fortifying it in part with the strength that had always been her own.

"You!" He took a single step toward her, the menace in his face growing. Then it gave way to puzzlement. "You are not—" he began and then checked himself. "No matter what you are—you do not serve him. But it may be that, of all this company, you can best stand against him. There is that in you which is a natural barrier to the forces at our command. I would suggest, Candace Naldamak, that this one"—he pointed deliberately to Tallahassee—"is best suited of all your people to front Khasti."

Herihor was on his feet. "Who commands here, stranger? Who are you to tell us whom to risk? You speak to us as a general speaks to a first recruit, and we are not for your ordering—"

"Your manner," interrupted the Candace, "does not impress itself well upon my officers. I will accept your warnings as the truth, but our battle plans remain ours—"

He was gone!

"What!—" Herihor's weapon came up, but all he faced was empty air.

"Where did he go?" One of the generals appealed to Jayta, as if she alone might have some answer to the riddle. "You knew him, or his like, Daughter-of-Apedemek. What is he then, and that other devil, making his mischief within Napata itself? Or is this some secret too great for our minds."

"It is an old secret, Nastasen, and one I have no right to share. But this much I say—his kind were known to the first men who were of Khem. And for some generations there was intercourse between our ancestors and such. Then they were gone, but they left us that knowledge upon which all our long history and learning is built. As for how he went—he may not have been here in flesh at all. They were able, legend tells us, to project images of themselves for long distances—"

"The wraiths?" asked Tallahassee.

Jayta frowned. "No, those wraiths which both aided and beset you are born out of the wickedness of Khasti. They are—or were—once people of our own kind, sent into a non-world for purposes of Khasti—a world into which they are imperfectly sealed, so that their thoughts and longing can reach through, if they can build up energy to do so by drawing it from us. Whether with the going of Khasti they can be restored—that even I do not know."

"If Khasti can also wink out after this manner," observed General Shabeke, "it would seem that our task is that much the greater. Perhaps the sooner we start upon it, the better."

"It has been near a day since Ashake came out of New Napata. We cannot be sure if Khasti knows where she is now. It would seem, that, in spite of his boasted power, he could not search the palace, or he would have hunted you down there, Sister. So there may be a few limits yet on the power he would seize. I think that the Nomarchs Idieze summoned have not yet proclaimed Userkof, Emperor, either. Thus it is better that we move as soon as possible. My lords,"—Naldamak spoke to the generals—"marshal the forces you have selected. I trust you have picked men who cannot be troubled too much by these 'wraiths.' Make sure to tell them what Ashake believes, that these lurkers in the invisible have good reason to hate Khasti; that one, at least, served the Princess in her great need. Ashake . . . Jayta . . ."

Naldamak paused. "I do not send others where I do not go. We shall head directly for the inner palace. I and half my guard shall ascend the secret stair into my own chambers. There I shall show myself. And—"

"I shall go to the laboratory." Though again Tallahassee had no intention of saying that, the words came from her lips. "Yes," she waved aside the protest in Herihor's face. "This stranger has said that I can stand best against Khasti. So be it—"

Naldamak's hand hovered over the Key and the Rod. "Take this then, Sister." She pushed the Key in Ashake's direction. "It is the symbol of all your learning. Thus it may profit you in this hour."

"I go with her." Jayta raised the lion mask from where it had rested beside her stool. "As Daughter-of-Apedemek I have certain powers of my own, as Khasti shall discover."

"So be it." The Candace nodded. "Let darkness be well advanced and we go."

Tallahassee had never thought to be returning through the noisome ways of the sewer, yet here she came, and at the head of no small company, with Naldamak herself between some of her guards not far behind, and Jayta at her very shoulder.

They had an abundance of light now, and though the girl watched carefully for any seeming curdling of the air to announce the presence of the wraiths, it would seem they no longer hunted.

They passed beneath the well which led upwards, and there they shed a full half of their force, the generals leading their men in that climb that should bring them out well within the walls of Napata. If they could force an exit through whatever topped off that well, excellent. If not they were to descend again and take the palace way. But their planned strategy was for simultaneous attacks from without the palace and within.

"This is a strange road." Jayta's voice sounded hollowly from within her mask. Ashake-Tallahassee wondered whether the mask filtered out some of the horrible stench. They went slowly, being careful of their footing.

But the added light and the company lightened the passage for her.

Finally they reached the foot of the stair that led to the Candace's suite and here two of the guards went to work, prying out the stones to open the way fully. Naldamak's hand fell on Tallahassee's arm.

"Good fortune be with you, Sister. This is a harsh gamble we take, not only with our own lives, but with Amun as well. Should we fail, Amun falls. Use the Key as you must, so will I use the Rod."

"And good fortune go with it," Tallahassee had wit enough to answer. Even Ashake memory could not give her a feeling of closeness to this resolute woman. From early childhood their lives had been lived apart. But that she could trust Naldamak, of that Tallahassee was very sure. In time she must trust her with the last secret of all—that there was no longer an Ashake.

With Jayta, three of the Amazon guard, and two men Herihor had insisted she take, Tallahassee sought Khasti's own stronghold. It was on the way there that she met the wraiths.

She heard a small gasp from Jayta, who raised her hand, her fingers crossed, in a certain way. Tallahassee swung up the Key, its natural radiance lost in the torch light. But it felt warm within her hand as if it now broadcast energy of a sort she could not understand, even with Ashake knowledge.

There was no movement, only that feeling of being hemmed in, as if invisible fingers plucked at their clothing, pulled at their hair, tried in every way to draw their attention. Ashake spoke without turning her head.

"These are those of which you were told," she said softly. "They can do you no harm. Perhaps they may be persuaded to aid us in some manner."

There were no answers from those who followed her, but she could sense their uneasiness at such company.

And she gave their courage high rating as they moved on, their boots ringing faintly on the ancient stone, with a firmness suggesting it would take more than what the wraiths manifested now to deter them from their purpose.

Unfortunately, something more just *might* lie ahead. What safeguards Khasti was able to throw about the center of his activity, the girl did not know, but he might have armed himself since her own escape.

Catching sight of the stairs, she passed the order to extinguish their torches. Climbing those stairs, they paused to listen for any sound from ahead. The wraiths were part of their company. Still they gave no sign of wishing to communicate. Perhaps they, too, waited to be sure Khasti had prepared no ambush.

Step after very cautious step the two women went up and on, the men following them. Without the torches, the Key shone with its own particular force as Ashake came into the hall, Jayta one pace behind. She had expected to see some light perhaps from the door of the laboratory, but if it were occupied the door must be firmly closed.

Whispering that what they sought lay now just a little ahead, Tallahassee edged close to the wall so that her shoulder brushed its surface as she went. It could not be much farther. No—there in the light of the Key she saw its smooth panels. But there was no sign of any opening latch. It might as well have been sealed like the stones that had earlier choked the other way.

Tallahassee slipped the palm of one hand along the surface, up and down to the length of her arm in both directions. There was nothing she could catch hold of. And when she pushed, first gently, and then with much more force, it remained immobile.

There remained the Key. She had not put it to any such test. She had used only the Rod before. But if it *were* a key, than what better way might she employ it? Concentrating on what she held, she raised the cross, clutching it by the loop at the top, and advanced its foot to the surface of the door as if she were in truth fitting a key to a lock. At the same time she felt Jayta's hand close about the arm that held the Key and from that touch poured a force to match her own, so that their united wills fed the ankh.

There followed a burst of sparks—though not such a great flare as the Rod had brought from the cage in which Khasti had earlier pent her. Then—the defensive barrier that had held the door was gone in an instant. Under her touch it swung open, so she was able to send it spinning back against the inner wall, two of the guard crowding up to shield both her and the Priestess from any waiting attack, with their own bodies if need be.

But there was no one inside. Tallahassee could see the cage still standing, the burnt-out hole in its side. And there were all the rest of the many things that crowded the tables, lined the walls. Yet something was missing. Tallahassee tried to remember what.

In a moment she understood. This was a deserted workplace, nothing bubbled, seethed, nor clicked. The activity she had seen before had ceased. Did that mean that Khasti had fled, having had some notice of their coming? Tallahassee did not believe that, rather that he had transferred his activities elsewhere. What remained here might now be valueless but they certainly would render all of it unusable.

"Be careful, my Princess," Jayta said as if she had read the girl's thoughts. "There may still be much that is harmful. We must move with caution since we do not understand."

Tallahassee accepted the prudence of that warning. But how *could* they understand? Or beware of harmful things they had never seen before? In her own time and world she had only the slightest knowledge of chemistry or physics. What she could draw upon as a warning was very limited.

"The Key will tell us." Again Jayta prompted her.

Ashake-Tallahassee advanced to the nearest table, her hand bearing the Key outstretched. Twice during her slow progress, while the guards kept watch at the doorway, the Key moved in her grasp, against her will, pointing down like a diviner's rod. Once it was above a small box of metal and again above a beaker of turgid yellow liquid. Each time Jayta took what was so indicated and carried it to the broken cage, setting her spoil within. Two more boxes and a rod, not as long as the talisman but rather like it in some ways, save that it lacked the lion mask, were added to those others before they were done.

Then Tallahassee called two of the guard to her while the others kept watch.

"Destroy," she ordered and pointed to the tables.

They smashed and splintered all into bits, moving rapidly along. There was a case like a file against the wall and from this Tallahassee herself tore the contents, sheets of tough paper covered with figures and diagrams foreign to her. These she hurled into the cage until they were heaped high about the objects the Key had marked as dangerous. For she knew now how to put an end to those and maybe the whole of this devilish chamber.

"Out—all of you! Back toward the Candace's stair and do not linger!"

"What are you doing?" Jayta asked, as the well-trained troops did as they were bid.

"I would see if Khasti's place of torment can still be used! Get you also to the door, Daughter-of-Apedemek. For what I may loose here might be a grave danger. And take you this." She pushed the Key into the priestess's hands.

Jayta backed away, she was at the door now. Tallahassee's hands went to those four buttons on the front of the box that had controlled the cage. It might be in breaking out of that prison she had also broken this. But she could try.

Her fingertips spread and punched—hard.

There was a glow on the wires of the cage at the back where they were still intact. She leaped back, pushing Jayta before her, to reach the outer wall.

"The stairway—let us make the stairway!" she cried out, catching the priestess's hand in a hard grip and hurrying her along.

$\mathcal{T}$HEY were well down on the stairs leading to the lower level, hearing the clatter of the guards' boots on the stone before them and seeing the beams of their torches, when the answer to Tallahassee's reckless gesture came. There was a roar of sound and a fierce burst of light from behind. The thick walls about them shook.

Both women took the last few stairs in leaps they would not have attempted earlier. The sound had deafened them, but Tallahassee waved the guard on and they plunged ahead to the second stairway leading to the Candace's chambers. Here they had to climb in single file and she came last, panting and dizzy from the shock of the explosion.

At the top they found Naldamak and Moniga. Sela was at the outer chamber door, listening. Tallahassee saw Naldamak's lips move as if she asked some question, and she had to shake her head.

"The noise—I am deaf," she said. "But we have destroyed, I believe, much that Khasti could have used against us."

She dropped, gasping for breath, on the end of the Candace's bed. Sela brought her a goblet of water and she drank thirstily.

The curtains had been drawn back from the windows opening onto the private garden so a night wind, scented by flowers, felt soothing against her hot face and arms. It was good to be here, to have another making the decisions.

Slowly her hearing came back.

There was a clamor in the halls—a duller roar from the city. Naldamak stood by one of the garden windows, her head tilted a little as she listened and perhaps so judged what might be happening from the very waves of sound. Tallahassee saw her lips move and this time caught a whisper of what she said.

"The Temple is free—Zyhlarz has spoken to us—"

An Amazon came swiftly through the outer chamber, saluted the Candace. "Sun-in-Glory, the gate barriers have been broken. But those of the Elephant are strong."

"If I show myself," Naldamak's answer came swift, "then they will be in open rebellion, and I do not think that after that they will find they have any cause."

"Glory—" The Amazon tried to step before her. "You are but one. A single blow, sent with ill fortune arming it, can bring you down. We are not enough to protect you—"

"There are those and that which none of these can face," the Candace returned. "We go to the Temple by the inner way."

Jayta's lion mask nodded in support and Tallahassee arose reluctantly. This was Ashake's work, but the memory now swelled in her so she could not resist.

Amazons closed about Naldamak and her two companions. They threaded halls, twice seeing dead lying crumpled against the walls. Their forces had met opposition here even in the heart of Naldamak's palace. Down another flight of stairs—in the distance shouting, the crackling fire of weapons. Then they entered the private way to the Temple, the way that Khasti had closed.

The Candace was running now, and Tallahassee had hard work to keep up with her, tired as she was and still partly dazed by the destruction in the laboratory.

But when they reached the other end of that corridor they found others before them. The Amazons of the guard pushed past Naldamak to form a wall of defense of their own bodies, using their weapons to pick off those who wheeled in shocked surprise to meet them. It would seem that, Khasti's invisible barrier having failed, he had sent men of the deep south, those who had never owned the belief of Amun, to hold in the priests.

Beyond those fighters Tallahassee saw one body wrapped in temple white—a white now dappled with scarlet. But the Amazons were finding targets, too. And Tallahassee, moved by Ashake's horror at what might happen, threw herself at the Candace, bearing her to the floor of the passage even as a flash of light passed over their heads, the discharge of a weapon new to her.

The Amazons plunged on, their battle screams rising above the sound of the weapons. It was the very fury of the women, whose fabled ferocity had been a legend for generations, that must have shaken the barbarians, battle-thirsty as they were. They went down in a struggling, heaving mass beneath the sheer weight of the maddened women.

The skirmish was over before it had scarcely begun. But three of the Amazons lay among the dead as the Candace and Tallahassee struggled to their feet.

"Blood in the Temple!" cried Jayta. "What blasphemy have they wrought here?"

"Evil," replied Naldamak. She looked to the Amazons. "Sworn Swords, what have I to say to you who have served me with life and death. Sisters in battle are you."

"Glory," their captain, nursing an arm from which blood flowed, replied, "it is our right to make smooth your path. There is no honor in doing one's duty. But it would seem"—she nodded toward the dead priest beyond—"that those of evil have already made an entrance here. I beg of you, go with care—"

"That I not undo all you have wrought? Yes. A life that has been bought by the blood of friends must not be thrown away. But within lies that which can end this slaughter."

They went on into the lower floor of the Temple warily, the Amazons scouting ahead. Naldamak spoke to Tallahassee and Jayta.

"There is no welcome. Do you not feel it? There is silence where there should be the force about us."

Ashake memory provided fear. Yes, to those of the Blood, of the Talent, there should have been an instant sense of coming home, of companionship, when they entered. Were—had Khasti brought death to all here? No rebel, not even a southern barbarian, would have dared such a thing. They had their own gods and sorcerers, but many feared with a healthy fear the Power of the Temple, alien though it might be to them.

Jayta held up her hand. "Do not seek!" she commanded. "Such a thought call could be a warning. We must go ahead in body only, keeping our minds closed."

They had come to the foot of the steps that led to the great central chamber, the very heart of the Temple. Tallahassee saw now, that, in Naldamak's hold, the Rod had become a staff of shining glory, producing a bright fire. And the Key Jayta held blazed high in answer.

The Candace turned at the foot of the stairs to face the Amazons.

"Sisters, here we part, for none but those of the Power may enter the inner way—not because of any need for secrecy, but because you, yourselves, would be burned by the fire that dwells herein and that only initiates can stand."

"Glory," protested the captain, "if the barbarians have come this way before you—"

"Then they are already dead or mindless," returned Naldamak. "This is of the Power. I forbid you on your Oaths to follow."

The captain looked as if she would raise a second protest, but Naldamak was already ascending the stair and Tallahassee fell in on her left, a step behind, Jayta on her right.

On the three climbed, alone, and all the while they listened, with their minds and their bodies rather than their ears. It could well be that they were ascending into a place of death. For what the Candace had said in warning was the truth, no one not prepared to stand the emanations of this place could live within the strength of the force that generations upon generations of calling upon the Talent had built here. Like the Rod and the Key, it was a reservoir, but a much greater one, of all the Power they had drawn upon.

They stepped out into the vast chamber. The very walls here were alight with ripples of energy. And by that light they saw those whom they had come to seek. A dozen men and women, white robed, mostly old. And to their fore, Zyhlarz himself, his dark face thinner, sharpened, and yet masterful.

Facing him—Khasti!

And at that moment Tallahassee sensed what was going on. They were engaged in a silent duel. The stranger out of nowhere had shielded his mind by some secret of his own, and between his hands was a circle of brilliant shining metal, the focus of what he sought to use to batter down the defenses of the Temple company.

They were matched so evenly, power thrust against power, that they seemed nearly dead to any metal probing. Nor did any face in that silent company of priests or priestesses change as Naldamak and the others came swiftly up behind Khasti's back.

The Candace held the burning rod now as a hunter might hold a lance, bringing it near shoulder high. And she was edging to the right of the immobile Khasti as if she would come even with him before she attacked.

She stopped and her two followers drew level with her. Jayta, holding up, heart high, the blazing Key, reached out her other hand and touched Naldamak's shoulder, giving good room to the Rod. Ashake's memory moved Tallahassee to do the same on the Candace's left.

It was like thrusting one's hands into a fire. There was heat in the flesh she touched, enough to nearly make Tallahassee jerk back her fingers. Now followed a drain from her own body, into Naldamak's.

At the same moment Khasti turned his head, though they had come noiselessly across the pavement. His eyes widened but he did not move.

Naldamak cast the Rod. It was a clean, well-aimed throw, passing through the ring of metal that Khasti held.

He threw back his head and laughed. "Not so easily do you win, Mistress of Magic."

"Stranger—your time here is finished. Choose death or go—"

"What death, Candace? Look to your Rod—it dies."

It was true. The Rod on the floor of the Temple had faded in brilliance as the coals of a fire will subside into grey and powdered ash. But there was no horror or fear on Naldamak's face.

"The Soul of Amun dies not, stranger." She held out her hand and the Rod arose from the floor, returned to her. Once in her grasp it flowered again with the same brilliance, yet Tallahassee felt the drain of her energy into the Queen's increase even as that brilliance grew.

"With this"—Khasti held the ring a fraction higher as if so to draw all their attention—"I can drain your 'soul' again and again and yet not be harmed."

"Daughter-of-Apedemek"—it was Zyhlarz's resonant voice that cut across Khasti's arrogant words—"whom have you brought with you into this place?"

He pointed into the air between Khasti and the Candace. Tallahassee could see the curling of the air, even though she had not yet felt the presence of the wraiths.

"Ask of them who and what they are, Son-of-Apedemek," Jayta replied. "They sought us in darkness, but they seek another more eagerly."

Again Khasti laughed. "They are my discarded tools, priest. To such can I reduce men. They served me, not too well. Now they would come to beg life once again. In their weakness they cannot harm me."

"Opener of Forbidden Gates," Zyhlarz answered him, "perhaps you have opened one too many."

There were three writhings in the air. They moved to box Khasti in on three sides. But he shrugged and smiled.

"I am not one to be driven from my goal by ghosts— nor by such 'Knowledge' as you cling to, old man. The Talent has run very thin, has it not? And my machines can best it in the end."

Tallahassee raised her own voice then:

"Akini!" she called. "I name your name, I give you what I have to offer . . ."

She held out the hand that had hung by her side, but she did not break contact with the Candace and through her with Jayta. One of the troublings in the air, the one behind Khasti, swooped closer.

"She has named a name!" Zyhlarz's voice swelled through the lofty hall. "Let hers be the Power!"

Just as energy had drained from her as Naldamak had wrought with the Rod—seemingly to no purpose—now it came flooding into her.

Her flesh tingled along the length of her slender body. She could feel a stirring on her scalp as if her clipped hair moved, each strand rising to discharge some force.

Something touched her outheld palm—so cold that it was like a thrust of pain following on the stroke of a knife. But Tallahassee held steady. And from that touch, even as had happened in the cage, a substance arose, milked out of her, absorbed by the thing in the air.

She saw Khasti half wheel, turn his circuit in her direction, but between him and her those two other disturbances of the air slid into place, so that his figure wavered before her eyes. But she did not drop her hand and the thing that fed on her strength continued to draw nourishment.

What was forming in the air bore no resemblance to a manlike form though that had been what she expected to see. Rather it was a serpent, ever thickening, ever pulling on her strength, draining not only herself but her companions also. Now, dimly, she could hear a rising chant from Jayta, saw from the corner of her eyes to the right that the Priestess was using the flashing Key to draw lines in the air, lines that glowed dimly and hung even after the Key withdrew.

Tallahassee thought, with a stab of fear, that her strength was being sapped past the point of no return. Yet that thing she had allowed to fasten on her did not abate its sucking. Had she condemned them all to failure?

"Akini!" That was Zyhlarz's call. "The door has been made ready—do you come through!"

The snake-thing loosed its hold from the girl's palm and her hand dropped weakly of its own volition to her side. She could see, even without turning her head, that there was indeed a doorway sketched upon the air.

But Khasti, his lips flattened against his teeth, his eyes showing a trace of madness, was raising his circlet, not aimed any longer at the priests and priestesses he had held so long at bay, but rather as if he would focus whatever force he controlled through it on the door in the air.

"Akini!" After Zyhlarz's call, her own voice sounded very weak and thin, as if it came not from her lips and throat but from a far distance.

The serpent coiled in the air, looping as if it rejoiced to own even this much of a form. But neither it nor the whirling wraiths made any attempt to go through that opening Jayta had provided for them. A door to here from *there* wherever there might be. Yet they did not come.

Instead the whorls kept guard between Khasti and the three he menaced. And the serpent thing—it launched at him as might a rope sent flying on Tallahassee's own world to ensnare a wild steer. It lifted itself above the level of his hands and the circlet, making for his head. He tried to dodge, dropped the thing he held, raising his arms to beat off the serpent.

But it was not to be denied. Wreathing itself around his head, it blotted out his features, covered his face instantly. He tore at it with no effect, staggering forward. Now the whorls ranged themselves on either side so that when he stumbled and wavered, he seemed to bounce from one to the other, they keeping him upright and urging him on. It was he who they hurried, blinded, perhaps suffocating under the serpent folds, into the door Jayta had opened.

He took one step and then another—and—was gone! The door vanished even as he passed through, leaving an eerie feeling of emptiness in the chamber, as if something had been closed, drawing with it a part of their lives in a way Tallahassee could not describe even to herself.

"But—I thought they wanted to come through to us," she said blankly. The Temple people were hurrying forward. "Why did they not come through?"

"Perhaps they could not. They had been so long exiled to that existence. What they wanted more," Jayta said slowly, "was him who had sent them there."

"Then—he will be a wraith . . . " Tallahassee could see the peril of that. She had felt the danger from those others, and they had been weaklings in strength of purpose when compared to the stranger out of the desert. What if he returned so to haunt them?

"They closed the door, Daughter." Zyhlarz was beside her. "You had the courage to treat with them after a fashion, and they have now removed him who alone had the power to destroy everything we are and have done."

"He was—" Jayta said, but Zyhlarz held up his hand in warning.

"Let it not be spoken aloud as to what he was. Such knowledge lies buried in the past and well buried. It is enough he was not of our flesh or of our world."

"There are those who have come seeking him," Naldamak said then.

"They will have their own way of knowing that he is gone. And on such a journey as even they are not ready to face. Time and space may be conquered by man— there remain other dimensions we dare not venture into if we would remain human."

Tallahassee sat in the Candace's garden. The city which had been in turmoil was now patrolled by loyal guards. Also the Temple was open so that there flowed out of it a peace that could soothe inflamed minds and quiet restless spirits.

Restless spirits! Since the vanishing of Khasti she had found herself at intervals watching the air, listening, sending out that inner sense of which Ashake made so much to test for alien thought, an alien wraith. Was it true that when Khasti had been swept away, by the "tools" he had despised, he had indeed been sealed from this world? He had been summarily thrown into another space-time even as she had been in the ruins of ancient Meroë?

Another space-time . . .

She was Tallahassee tonight as she sat here alone in the dusk. Though her begrimed uniform had been changed for the silken robes of her borrowed personality, a wig of ceremony covered her head, she was *not* Ashake!

She thought of what Jayta had hinted in the last council they had held a few hours ago—that Khasti had not come out of time but out of space. That the fabric of Khem itself in the earliest days had been born of the experiments made by intelligences not of this world, and that their blood and gifts had lingered on in certain descendants, to become part of another path of knowledge, turning inward. Thus, those whose far-off forefathers had known the stars now chose rather to know themselves, perhaps better than any of their species had done before.

They had seen no more of that second stranger. Perhaps they could believe it was true he and those he represented had known of their quarry's fate and gone their own ways thereafter.

But there remained Tallahassee Mitford, who was not of Amun and who should now go her way, too. She had seen Jayta open a door through which Khasti had vanished. But she did not want to be caught in the non-life of a wraith. If there was a door possible between her world and this it must be real—

"You think strange thoughts, Royal Lady."

Tallahassee raised her eyes from the shadowed path at her feet. Jayta and Naldamak, and with them, Herihor, one arm in a sling to bear witness that he was not Prince General to order and not lead his men into battle, and lastly, Zyhlarz, stood there. Now to these four she must speak the truth, no matter what would come of it.

"I am not your Royal Lady. You"—she spoke directly to Jayta—"know who and what I am. Now I ask you, since I have served your purpose, to let me go."

Jayta must have shared her knowledge with the others. Even in this dim light Tallahassee could see that none showed surprise.

"My daughter—" Zyhlarz began, when she interrupted.

"Lord Priest, I am not your daughter, nor one of your kind!"

"No, you are less and more—"

"Less and more? How can one be both?"

"Because we are each shaped from our birth, not only by the blood and inheritance that lies behind us, but also by those we love and by whom we are loved in turn, by the knowledge given to our thirsty minds, to the learning of ourselves. You are not Ashake—though Ashake, in part, has become you—nor can you indeed ever tear her out of your memory and thought. But you are also yourself and so have different qualities—which are yours alone."

"Can you send me back?" She asked that bluntly.

"No." Jayta did not wear her lioness mask now and in the dusk her face looked very tired and drawn.

"Why?" She had seen the priests do things she would have believed impossible. "You have the Key and Naldamak has the Rod—and you," she spoke now to Zyhlarz, "have all the learning of the Upper Way wholly yours."

"There must be an anchor to draw one," Jayta said. "When Akini was sent through, and those others—the nameless ones—they were anchored upon the power of the Rod—first to remove and conceal it. Then the Rod was taken into a place where such like it had once been. When the Key was stolen, it could be borne there also because the Rod was there to draw it.

"But when Ashake went to search, in turn, her hand upon the Rod and Key, her right to hold and call upon them, was such that it drew you also. For you were—in your world—the one whom she would have been had she lived in your time and place—you were equal within you. Do you think otherwise the memories of Ashake could have been given you? Now there is no anchor existing beyond. When Akini and those others were not drawn back in time—you saw what they became. For in your world, it would seem, they had no counterparts—so they were lost between. Perhaps Khasti has so been lost. It is our hope that his like does not exist elsewhere.

"Ashake died because she could not draw her other existing self through without giving the full energy of her body. There is no door left for you because nothing lies there to fasten upon."

"You are Ashake and you are more . . ." Herihor spoke for the first time.

Naldamak held out both her hands. "The Prince General speaks the truth, Sister. Was this other world of yours so beloved to you that you cannot live without it? If there was a dear love existing there, perhaps that could pull you. But if that were true the Son-of-Apedemek would have known. Thus I say to you, Sister—you are not less than Ashake in our eyes. Look upon us now and read the truth!"

Tallahassee's searching glance went from face to face of those who shared her secret. Ashake—all Ashake, more or maybe less—but never a wraith out of time. Here she was real, welcomed. She took the hands of Naldamak offered her and accepted all else that was in their faces and hearts as they looked upon her.

The Universe of Science Fiction